Past
To Die For

BY

ALYSIA S. KNIGHT

Heart Dreams
PRESS

Past to Die For

By Alysia S. Knight
Published by Heart Dreams Press
Copyright © 2013 Alysia S. Knight
Cover design: by Kelli Ann Morgan @
www.inspirecreativeservices.com

ISBN:-1-942000-29-4
ISBN-13:978-1-942000-29-7

To those who don't let anything keep them down,
keep on smiling and working on your future.

All my love,
Alysia S. Knight

Chapter One

"This couldn't be happening." Jana Hamilton muttered to herself as she pushed back from her desk and headed for her boss's office. She hoped there were some missing entries. Otherwise, something was terribly wrong with the ledger.

She shook her head in frustration. *Just last minute figures for an early morning meeting. Everyone knew good, little Jana wouldn't have any other plans, so she could stay late and finish. Well, this time, she did mind. She had a life, too.*

Jana ignored the darkness, striding down the hallway. Light came from around the door left cracked open. "Mr. Mur…" Her boss's name died on her lips as the door swung open with her knock.

Two men stood in the middle of the room. For a second, Randolph Murdock faced his client, Cameron Kellerman. The next instant, he dropped to the floor. The same crimson which covered the knife in Kellerman's hand, spread across Mr. Murdock's pristine white shirt.

The shock that held Jana frozen evaporated as Kellerman's gaze rose to meet hers. The satisfied look on the killer's face disappeared, and Jana knew she was next to die. Turning and fleeing didn't enter her mind. She just ran.

Behind her, the door banged back against the wall. Footsteps sounded frightfully close as Jana rounded the corner, praying someone would be there. Preferably a very big policeman, but no one was there. No one else was in the building, just her, her dead boss, and his murderer.

She passed a tall wastebasket and tipped it over, hoping to trip the killer like it always did in the movies. No stumbling sounded behind her. Heavy breathing spurred her on. Jana dodged the secretary's desk and headed for the stairway when Kellerman leapt over the desk. A hand caught the back of her collar, digging it into her neck as he pulled her to the ground.

I don't want to die. The words roared in her mind.

She swung back, hitting hard.

The knife kept coming.

Jana threw up her hands and felt the blade bite into the side of her palm. She deflected the knife away. Drawing up to her legs, she kicked out, sending the man falling backwards.

She hauled herself up by the corner of the desk. Frantically, she grabbed the telephone and threw it at Kellerman as he started to rise. With a curse, he fell back. The only other thing on the desk was the computer, which she shoved at him, then turned and ran.

Jana hit the stairway door at a full run. She'd just made it down the first flight when she heard the door open above. By the next flight, he'd gained enough for her to know she wouldn't make it to the bottom before he caught her. She pulled open the stairway door.

A reception desk, much like the one they'd fought around two flights above, was the only thing she saw. Jana scrambled around the huge desk, and crawled underneath, pulling the chair in tight. She scrunched in deeper and tried to take a couple deep breaths to still her labored breathing.

When the door opened, she held her breath, afraid of making a sound. The door closed. The thick carpet made it impossible to tell where the man was.

Please don't let him find me became a mantra running through her mind. She fought to keep in the sob that choked to get out. Funny, as a child she'd considered herself a pro at hide-and-seek. But now the stakes were different, and there was no home free.

The sound of another door opening around the corner gave Jana the incentive she needed. Sliding the chair to the side, she peeked around the corner. The hallway was clear. Scrambling out, she ran to the elevator and hit the down button, leaving a bloody smear behind. She ducked into the stairway, easing the door closed before heading up.

At the next floor, she froze and pressed back against the stairwell. Below her the door banged back against the wall, but the killer didn't even glance her way as he raced down the steps. When the heavy metal door clanked shut below, she pressed open the door behind her and ducked inside.

Jana leaned against the wall and fought to take in several deep breaths. She raised her hand to her mouth and tried to catch the escaping sob, which still slipped free when, for the first time, she noticed the blood on her hand. Panic threatened to overcome her, but she forced it down. Jana drew a couple of deep breaths, placed her hand tight against her body, and locked her arm over it.

Blood immediately soaked through her shirt. She ignored it, heading past the reception desk. As she raced down the hallway, she tried all the door handles hoping to find one unlocked, careful, now, not to leave a trail of blood. Finally, a knob turned. She pushed the door open and dodged inside.

"Please," she whispered as she ran to the phone and snatched it up. The silence was deafening. The connection wasn't there.

"No," Jana cried, looking around and realizing the office was devoid of all personal belongings. It was vacant. That was why it was unlocked. She almost sank to the floor in despair.

Where was Kellerman? Could she risk leaving the

room? She had to find a phone. She had to call the police. She had to get help.

Jana went to the door and cracked it open enough to see into the hall. She'd just decided it was safe and started out when the bell from the elevator shattered the silence. Jana's heart jumped. She pulled back and pressed the door closed. Her hands fumbled with the lock, clicking it into place.

As she stared at the door, the faint sound of knobs being rattled down the hallway reached her. One by one, the sound drew closer. Her breath caught as she waited. It seemed forever, then the knob jiggled.

Jana fought back a sob, praying the lock would hold. She caught her bottom lip between her teeth hard enough she tasted blood, but the sob didn't break free. The door groaned from the pressure against it. Then it was still. Farther down the hall, another knob rattled.

Jana's heart pounded with relief, but she couldn't let go of her fear. Placing one foot behind her, she moved backward until she bumped into the desk. Still afraid to take her eyes from the door, she edged around it. Her heart pounded painfully in her chest.

Backing up again, she came up against the wall. Unable to go farther, her legs gave out, dropping her to the floor. She barely caught the sob that wanted to slip out. She fought to get control of herself but couldn't get past the image of blood spreading over Mr. Murdock's always pristine white shirt.

She started to clinch her fists and sucked in a breath. Pain burned in her hand bring the injury to her attention. Using the corner of her blouse, Jana applied pressure to the wound as she huddled in the darkness, afraid any minute the killer might return.

Time passed agonizingly slow. Her mind wandered. When she heard the door handle rattle again, she was so surprised the squeak slipped out before she could stop it.

"Mackey, did you hear something?" The unfamiliar voice came through the door.

"No, the floor's clear."

Jana could barely make out the words.

The voices were followed by the crackle of what sounded like a police radio asking for an update. Jana pulled herself off the floor. On shaky legs, she stumbled across the room, opened the office door and tumbled into the arms of a startled young officer. The sobs she'd fought to hold at bay in the terrifying darkness broke free as what happened spilled out. The tears didn't stop when she had to start again and repeat everything to a detective.

Hours later, after the cut in her hand had been stitched, she was taken to the police station. Twice more she repeated her story before finally falling asleep on the couch in the captain's office.

The next morning, she sat on the same worn, plaid couch as she was informed that the government had been after Kellerman for a while. Her stomach turned.

"Miss Hamilton, you do understand what we're asking?" Jared Tanner, the prosecutor who'd come in to talk with her, asked.

All she could do was nod.

"And you're willing to testify?"

"Yes," she managed to get the word out.

"Thank you. I know you've been through a lot, but we really appreciate your help. We got close to getting Kellerman before, but our possible witness ended up dead. I'm telling you this so you will know how serious this is. We never thought we'd catch Kellerman doing his own dirty work."

Jana felt like she'd been punched.

"Don't worry. We're not going to let anything happen to you," he added in a hurry. "You're going to be taken into protective custody right now. You'll have round-the-clock guards. Only a handful of people will know your whereabouts." There was a knock on the door. Tanner looked up. "Speaking of which, that's them now."

He opened the door, motioning in the man and woman who stood there. The woman, U.S. Marshal Karen Fields, was slightly shorter than Jana's own five feet eight inches. She had chin-length, brown hair, and a pert little nose that took away some of the impact of her too serious eyes. Her partner, Jake Morgan, couldn't have been more opposite, a tall, burly Texan with silver-blond hair and laugh lines. An hour later, she left the police station with the Marshals and then things really fell into a haze.

സ്റ

After six weeks of being shuffled around, Jana still could hardly believe any of it could be happening to her. She stared blankly out the window at the prim little houses and tree-lined road.

"Okay darlin'. This is it. Home sweet home until the trial," U.S. Marshal Jake Morgan drawled, pointing out the window.

"This is the safe house?" Jana thought out loud as she jerked alert. She leaned forward to get a better look through the windshield. It was a lot different than the hotel they'd stayed at the first few nights and the condo they'd just left. The white house was small, with blue trim and flower gardens out front. A low hedge bordered the driveway that ran around the house to the backyard.

"Yup, I know it's not the Ritz, but it should be comfortable. It's fully stocked, but if there's anything your little heart desires, Karen or I can pick it up when we go out."

"No, it's fine. It just looks so – ordinary." Jana glanced back at Karen's car following them. Then again, who would have ever thought soft-spoken Karen was a Federal Marshal? Or that she, Jana Hamilton, ordinary, good-girl accountant would ever witness a murder.

"That's the idea." Jake turned the car onto the long

10

driveway that circled to the secluded backyard. He shifted into park but didn't cut the motor until his partner, Karen, pulled alongside. "I know we've done this before, but this is how it goes. You don't get out of the car until I get you."

Jana nodded as she watched Karen circle the yard before coming up behind the car. Jake popped the trunk. Karen lifted out Jana's single suitcase and headed for the back door, while Jake made his way around the car.

Jana clinched her fingers into the soft suede purse on her lap, unable to quell her nervous feeling. She watched Jake's eyes roam the yard as he reached down to help her out of the car. Purse in hand, Jana reached back for her overnight bag.

"No, leave it." Jake stopped her, tension filled his voice. "I'll get it later." After being around him for weeks, Jana could tell something had him on edge.

"Jake?"

"Let's get you inside." In answer, Jake clamped a large hand on her arm as he propelled her toward the back door.

Ahead, Karen slid the key into the lock at the same instant Jake turned and shoved Jana to the ground, while pulling his gun. Several shots rang out from the wooded slope behind the yard. Jake's gun thundered in return.

"Get to the house!" Jake punctuated the order with several more shots. Dirt kicked up near Jana's legs, spurring her into motion. Jana scrambled to her feet, focusing ahead on Karen, who had her gun out, firing toward the hillside as she pushed the door open.

Everything came apart as the house exploded. Jana found herself on the ground once more, this time with Jake's big body half covering hers.

"Are you all right?"

Through the ringing in her ears, she made out Jake's ever-present drawl. Jana's mind processed the question, but she couldn't seem to get the answer out of her shaken body. "Jana!" The sharp tone demanded a response.

"Yes ... yes. I think so."

In answer, two shots burst from Jake's gun as he shifted to his knees. "The car, now!"

Obeying, Jana scrambled to her feet. She turned to the car only to turn back as she heard Jake groan. "Jake."

He staggered to his feet. "Go!"

"You're shot." She reached for him.

"No, go."

"But ..." She felt him press the set of hard metal keys into her hand and close her fingers over them.

"To the car ... go ... go!" He drew a ragged breath then shoved her away, firing several more shots at the hillside. Jana was only three feet from the car when the next explosion knocked her to the ground. Her hands and knees stung as gravel bit into her skin. Pieces of wood and other debris rained down. Dust coated her, and pain rippled through every nerve, but her mind focused on the last words Jake had said, "car ... go". If she left, the killer wouldn't have any more reason to hurt Jake and Karen. It was her he wanted.

She fought to hold back a sob as she stumbled and crawled her way to the car. Jana pulled open the passenger door and climbed across. Praying, she shoved the key into the ignition and started the car before sitting up behind the wheel.

Jana stared out the window. The tidy white house with blue trim that had stood as a safe haven moments before was now a pile of rubble, licked by flames. There was no sign of Karen. Jake stood hunched. He shifted, looking directly at her and mouthed. "Go! Go!"

A sharp thud hit the hood, jerking Jana into action. She shoved the car in reverse and floored the accelerator. The car rocketed backward scraping along the shrubbery on the driver's side. Jana overcorrected, cutting across the lawn. She veered off the curb, barely missed a car parked across the street. Braking only enough to shift the car into drive, she bumped over the curb again before fleeing down the street.

Jana prayed the killer would follow her and prayed that he wouldn't. She didn't know where she was going. She just wanted to get away from the blood, the violence, and the horrible scenes running through her mind: Images of Jake, hunched and firing, blood covering his shirt. Karen just before the house exploded.

All the scenes tumbled together into the first night of terror when she'd witnessed her boss's murder. The night she had hidden, praying for help, for somewhere safe, but there was nowhere safe. No Jake. No Karen. No safe house. They were all gone, probably dead just like Mr. Murdock.

The sound of the low fuel indicator pulled Jana's thoughts back to the present. She looked around and realized she had no idea where she was. The terrain had changed. It was flatter and more barren. Just low hills dotted with cattle and sagebrush.

The sky had changed also. It was no longer bright and sunny. Now it was dull, cloudy and looked about to storm.

Jana realized she had no idea how long she'd been driving. Passing a mile marker, it told her a number, but no location. She looked nervously at the gas gauge that read almost empty as she drove on. Three more mile markers passed before she found a highway sign with a bucking bronco.

Wyoming. She was in Wyoming, but where? How far had she gone? Looking back down at the fuel gauge setting on the red line, she figured quite a ways since the tank had been full that morning. The next question was how far to a gas station, and could she make it?

Sixteen more miles down the highway, the town of Wilson Butte was a welcoming sight, but brought little relief to Jana's mind. It wasn't big, stretching ahead a dozen or so blocks. It did have several gas station signs though. Pulling into the first station she came to, Jana cut the engine. Wind whipped across the windshield bringing the first sprinkles of the coming storm.

Jana reached automatically for her purse and realized it was back on the ground where she'd dropped it when Jake pushed her down. Remembering the scene, she shuddered. But thinking of Jake also reminded her of the pocket he'd showed her under the seat. Inside was stashed money in case of an emergency.

Reaching down, she found the pocket. She slipped her fingers inside and made contact with an envelope. Pulling it out, she found five twenty-dollar bills.

Jana startled, jerking up as wind buffeted the car. Rain fell harder. A chill ran through her. She needed a coat. Jana shifted her weight to look over the seat back and flinched at the pain in her left leg. When she reached for Jake's jacket, she felt a matching pain in her shoulder, and realized that her body was no longer numb, and she hurt all over.

Ignoring the pain, she pushed the car door open. Cold wind and rain hit her. Jana forced herself to stand and struggled to pull on the jacket. It was awkward with the throbbing in her shoulder, but the chill in the air hurried her on.

Within minutes, the tank was full, and forty-five dollars was gone from her pocket. Jana wasn't any more certain what her next step should be. She had to have help. She just wasn't quite sure who to turn to.

She looked around trying to get her bearings. The café next to the gas station caught her eye. The building didn't boast anything special, though the lights inside beckoned warm and inviting. Moving the car into a parking place, she once more braved the cold. Inside the café, the heat hit her carrying a feeling of comfort in the air.

Along the counter, five men sat talking to an older woman wearing a waitress uniform. Three more men sat in one booth. A family sat in another. The men in the booth looked up, giving her a thorough onceover before returning to their conversation.

Jana slid into the booth spaced away from the two groups. Blissfully, it turned out to be directly over the heat vent. Closing her eyes, she soaked up the warmth.

"Feels good, doesn't it."

The voice startled her. Jana opened her eyes to a gray-haired waitress. Wrinkles lined the face, but it was still beautiful with kindness. Jana nodded, fearing if she tried to answer she'd break out in tears.

"Would you like a menu or just a coffee?" The woman studied her.

It took a minute for Jana to think. It'd been a long time since she'd eaten. Early that morning, they'd eaten breakfast before moving her to the new holding location. Jana felt her insides churn as memories hit her again. It was hard enough to keep the tears down, she knew there was no way her stomach could manage food. "May I have hot chocolate? I don't drink coffee."

"Sure, I'll be right back." The woman gave her a reassuring smile.

A minute later, she reappeared with the cup of creamy brown liquid. Jana managed a smile and wrapped her hands around the cup. She sighed at the warmth entering her body. It felt heavenly on her hands. She couldn't help but wonder if she would ever truly feel warm inside again.

Tears built up pressure. Jana closed her eyes, trying to keep the tears from spilling out. The only time she had been more frightened in her life was the hours she'd spent, sitting in the dark, waiting for the killer to find her.

Well, it wasn't dark, but the killer was still out there looking for her. He had found her today at the safe house. It sounded so impossible. Jake had told her that no one could find her there, that only a handful of marshals knew where she would be. But the killer had been waiting. He'd known. Someone had to have told.

Jana longed to put her head down and cry. Instead, she

forced herself to think. Jake had made her memorize a number in case of emergency. The thought of using it sent a wave of fear through her. Did the killer know it, too? Or would whoever informed the killer be the one on the other end of the phone.

Please, I need help, Jana cried again in her mind.

At the soft thump on the table Jana opened her eyes. A second cup of hot chocolate sat next to her hands. This one, unlike the cup she held, had steam rising from it. The waitress slid into the seat across from her.

"You might find this one warmer."

"Thanks," Jana managed a weak smile and slid her cup over. Accepting the new one, she took a sip.

"Dearie, are you all right?"

Jana nodded, still not sure if she trusted her voice.

"My name's Noma."

"Jana," she answered back automatically.

"Would you like to talk about it?" Concern radiated from the woman.

"No, I'm okay, really." Jana could tell the woman didn't believe that and really wanted to help. There was just no way.

Noma rose, for a minute she just stood there. "If you need anything …" she said then started to turn.

In that instant, Jana knew what she needed to do. "Wait!" As the woman turned back, Jana wavered. "Can …," she took a steadying breath, "can you tell me about the police chief here?"

"We're not big enough for a police department. We're under the sheriff's department."

"What's the sheriff like?" Another rush of anxiety raced through her.

"What are you asking exactly?" Noma slid back into the seat.

Jana swallowed down the lump in her throat before continuing. "Is he honest?"

"JT Termaine. He's as honest as the day is long. They don't come any better than that man. Listen, if you got a husband or boyfriend trying to hurt you, he'll help. He don't put up with that kind of thing."

Jana had to smile at her assumption. She must be looking pretty bad. "Can you tell me how to get to the sheriff's office?"

"Sure, it's just two blocks down the street on the right, but he's not there right now. One of his deputies, Monty or Gerald, should be there, though, and they can help."

Jana hesitated before, pressing on. "Can you tell me how to find the sheriff?"

The woman eyed her a moment then nodded. "Go down two blocks, at the same corner as the sheriff station, except take a left. Follow that road out of town six miles. There's a bridge about halfway. Be careful crossing it because it'll be slick with this storm. In fact, it would be better if you waited the storm out here. It looks to be a messy one. These late spring storms are nothing to be taken lightly."

Jana looked out the window. The darkened sky was ominous, but not as ominous as the killer after her. She shook her head and took another sip of the warm liquid to push back the chill. "I think I better go. Thank you." She reached into her pocket for her money, but the waitress held up her hand.

"It's on the house, the storm and all."

"I ... thank you."

"You're welcome, but you might want to reconsider waiting out the storm," the older woman cautioned her one more time.

Jana knew the warning was sound, but she was just too afraid to wait, so again she shook her head. "I'll drive carefully. Thank you for the help."

"Well, if anyone can help you, it'll be JT Termaine."

ೞಐ

17

Jana blinked her eyes rapidly to clear her mind from the dizzying effect of tunnel vision from the flecks of snow being blown at the windshield. The snow had begun to come down hard by the time she had made it to the corner, now she leaned forward, struggling to see out better. She eased up on the gas again, dropping her pace down to a crawl. Maybe she should've waited at the café.

It'd taken her nearly twenty minutes to reach the bridge, and then she was almost across it before she even realized she was on it. She kept going, counting the minutes. There had been no other cars on the road since she left town. Jana knew she had to be getting close. Pressing forward, she strained to see, afraid of driving right past.

The snow was coming down so heavy the headlights didn't seem to help. Nearly six inches had already accumulated on the road. Jana shivered, though the heater did a good job warming the car. She searched the side of the road for the sheriff's house. It had to be close. She hoped he would be able to help her. Her mind conjured up images of Andy Griffith.

Glancing out the side window, she prayed to see the turn or some kind of life. There was nothing but snow. Then, off in the distance, there was a faint light. Jana glanced back to the road then back off to the side. It was still there, barely visible through the snow and fading light, she could make out the outline of a house, barn and several other buildings.

Tears trickled down her cheeks as a profound joy filled her body. She turned back to the road, and her joy shattered.

"No!" Jana screamed as the form of a deer took shape out of the haze in front of the car. Instinct had her foot slamming on the brake before her mind could caution against the action. It was already too late. The car slid out of control.

Jana tried to push the panic down and steer into the

slide, but the next moment the wheel jerked in her hands as the car fishtailed and spun. The seatbelt dug into her shoulder as she was thrown forward then slammed against the side window as the car slid off the road. Her head smacked the window. Pain ricocheted through her head. The wild ride slowed, then blurred away as she lost consciousness.

捣

Cold, was the first conscious thought that pulled Jana to awareness; blackness was the second. Shifting her numb body brought dull pain, confusion, and then nausea. Closing her eyes, Jana rested her head back against the seat. Her insides settled, but the shivers that racked her body became more pronounced.

"I'm freezing." She heard the words and realized she said them aloud.

Common sense said you weren't supposed to leave your car and to wait for help. Unfortunately, she had nothing in the car to keep her warm. Looking at the darkness beyond the snow covered window, she knew quite a bit of time had already passed.

A sob caught in her throat. How ironic, twice she had a killer after her, and now she was going to die by freezing to death, sitting in a car. People said it was a painless way to go. Well, she didn't want painless. She wanted to feel the pains of life, like childbirth and growing old. She wanted to live!

Inside, she knew, if she wanted to live she had to have help, and if she wanted help, she'd have to go find it. Decision made, she reached for the door handle. Her first attempt to open the door was unsuccessful. Putting all her weight against it, Jana pushed. The door cracked open, admitting a chilling stream of cold air.

The exertion made her head begin to swim. Dizzying lights flashed before her eyes. Her body trembled.

After a moment slumped against the seat, her head

cleared. Jana turned, pressed her feet against the door and pushed. Lights again flashed, but with a groan from her and the car, the door opened halfway until it came up against the side of the ditch.

Wind and snow whipped inside hitting her face. Jana pulled back and took a couple deep breaths of the frosty air before she crawled out into the storm.

By the time she made it out of the ditch to the road, she was shivering violently. Jake's jacket did little to repel the snow. The material had already turned icy. Only the sight of the houselights through the storm gave her hope.

Crossing the road, she slid down the other slope. She stumbled over sagebrush hidden by the snow. Jana fell, sending spikes of pain ricocheting up her frozen arms. The sweet taste of blood from her cracked lip registered in her mind. Whimpering, she pulled herself back up, staggering against the wind.

The fence posed another problem. One of the barbs jabbed her hand, another caught her pants before tearing across her leg. After what seemed like an eternity, she collapsed on the ground on the other side.

Unable to stop herself, she gulped in great amounts of frozen air. The desire to curl up on the ground and sleep was strong. It almost won before Jana realized it would be a deadly error.

She forced herself to her feet. Focusing all her attention on the light, she set a goal to reach it. Each step was excruciating. It took all her will to put one foot in front of the other. The progress was agonizingly slow, but the light was getting closer.

The hole she stepped in was hidden in the snow. Before Jana knew what was happening, she was falling. She tried to catch herself with her arms, only to have them give way, letting her face be buried in the snow.

Tears froze to her cheeks. She managed to lift her head to brush at the snow on her face. The crushing weight of despair threatened to overwhelm her. She was so tired, frightened and cold. It was more than she could handle. No, she told herself, she could do it.

Jana pushed her head up higher, trying to make out the ghostly shapes of buildings through the storm. She focused on the shape of the large ranch house and the tauntingly, welcome lights. They were so close, but to her weary body and mind, they seemed an impossible distance.

She wrapped her arms around herself, huddling to the ground, but there was no warmth or comfort. With a cry, she struggled once more to her feet. Staggering, she made it to the fence around the yard. This time it was made of wood, and she was able to crawl between the boards.

Jana collapsed to the ground staring across a football field-sized yard. She knew there was no way she could make it. She had no strength. The next step took all her will. One more, she cried in her mind. One more. She refused to give up.

The next thing she knew, she tripped over the porch step. Unable to rise, she crawled up the stairs. With her last bit of strength, she staggered upright only to fall against the doorframe then slump against the door.

Her mind breached the etiquette of good manners as she struggled to turn the knob but couldn't get her fingers to grip it tight enough. Shielded slightly from the storm, she rested her head against the door for a second before raising her hand. Spears of pain exploded as her frozen fingers contacted with the wood. She forced her hand to knock over and over until she had no more strength to move her hand. Her arm fell limply to her side, and she slumped against the door.

Chapter Two

JT Termaine ran his fingers through his dark brown hair as he made his way down the hall. The flannel shirt he'd pulled on with a pair of faded jeans hung open. Four hours of sleep did little to make up for the thirty-six he'd gone without, but it was enough for food to become the primary need of his body. The smell of bread, cinnamon, and sugar lured him from sleep.

JT stepped into the living room, than jerked at the sound of something bumping against the house. He glanced out the window at the heavy snow falling. If there was such a thing as a day perfect for hot cinnamon rolls, it was today – hot chocolate, cinnamon rolls, and for once, letting his deputies handle all the problems.

The instant the thought crossed his mind, a knock sounded at the door. It was so faint that, if he hadn't been in the room, he would never have heard it. So faint that it almost shouted trouble had found him.

He did up half the buttons on his shirt before he opened the door. A blast of freezing air hit his body with shocking force, but it was nothing compared to seeing the woman there. Only an oversized, lightweight jacket protected her from the elements. Snow and ice clung to her.

"Help me." The weak words trembled out in a puff of cold from blue lips before the figure crumbled.

JT dove forward, catching her before she hit the ground. She made no movement as he swung her into his arms. The woman felt more like an ice cube against his body than a live human.

Shoving the door closed with his foot, he moved to the couch. "Maggie!" he yelled, grabbing the afghan from the back of the couch. He changed his mind and dropped it to first work the pair of soaked tennis shoes from her feet. He draped the afghan over her legs and feet. He started to take off the jacket, which proved a much more difficult task. "Maggie!" he yelled again. "Tyler!"

"JT Termaine, you sound more like your grandfather every day. As sheriff, you'd think you'd heard of disturbing the peace … Glory! What's that?" his aunt said, stepping from the kitchen.

"Not what, who."

"Dad?" Tyler, his nine-year-old son, came through the swinging door behind his great-aunt.

"Tyler, call Dr. Phillips. See if he can make it over here. Tell him we have a woman in her twenties, unconscious, with hypothermia." His son's lithe body was back through the kitchen door without asking any foolish or time consuming questions.

Owen Phillips had retired to the small ranch just a quarter mile down the road. But, like any good doctor in a rural area, retirement was never total, and they still made house calls.

"She's like ice. We have to raise her body temperature," JT said.

He knew Maggie understood there wasn't time to waste. Hypothermia was deadly, and the woman screamed of it. She needed to be treated fast before permanent damage was done. Hopefully, it wasn't too late already.

In silent communication, Maggie headed down the hall. JT scooped the woman up in his arms and headed after her. The water was already flowing into the tub when JT walked through his bedroom into the bathroom. Maggie stepped out of the way so he could kneel next to the tub.

Heedless of his shirt, he lowered the woman into the

water, clothes and all. The water was cold on his skin, but he knew it would almost be shocking to the iciness of hers. That was something they had to be careful of. They needed to raise her temperature, but not faster than her body could take, or they would send her into shock.

The woman showed no response. Concerned, he raised his fingers to her neck and felt for her pulse. "A little slow, but strong."

"Dad," Tyler appeared in the doorway. "Dr. Phillips said he was sure he could make it, but it would take him about ten minutes."

"Thanks, Ty."

"Is there anything else I can do?" There was anxiousness in his son's voice that JT knew was a need to help.

"Yeah, actually, can you start a fire in my fireplace? We'll need it really warm in there."

"Got it."

"Let's start adding a little warm water," Maggie said, reaching for the knob.

Several minutes passed quickly before Tyler appeared at the door again. "The fires lit. I'm going to watch for Dr. Phillips."

"Thanks," JT answered, not looking up.

"Tyler." Maggie stopped the boy. "Pull down the covers and get a couple spare blankets and put them on the foot of the bed."

"Yes, ma'am."

It was closer to twenty minutes, and they had warmed the water twice more before Dr. Phillips arrived.

"How are we doing in here?" He came bustling in the room followed by Tyler.

"We've had her warming since Ty called you, but she's still unconscious," JT answered.

"All right." Doc shifted past JT to go down on one knee. Grasping her hands, he studied them for a couple seconds before moving his examination to her face, neck then feet. "Good." He looked at the tattered knees of her soaked pants. "Why don't we keep her here while I cut her jeans away?"

"Tyler, why don't you go to the kitchen and wait." Maggie shooed him from the room.

Doc reached into his bag for a pair of scissors. He continued to talk as he went to work, cutting off the pants. "There's a car in the ditch just before your turn. That must be where she came from. I stopped to check it. There was no one else inside. By the way, I'd say there's no way we're going to get her to town."

"I figured that," JT answered. "I'm just glad you could make it."

"It was getting tricky. That'll do. Let's get her out of the water and see what we have. Can you lift her?"

With a nod, JT slid his arms under her body. Doc steadied her head as JT stood, and Maggie quickly draped a towel over the woman, then wrapped another towel around her hair.

"That's fine, let's move her to the bed," Doc directed, and together, they moved into the bedroom, now warmed by a large fire. Maggie moved ahead to spread one of the spare blankets out. As soon as JT lowered the woman down, Maggie bundled it around her.

"That should be fine." Doc took over again. "Maggie will you help me here?"

JT was relieved to be able to turn his back from the view of the woman lying in his bed. He tried to shake off the disturbing feeling that filled him, seeing her there. He didn't know what it was, but there was almost a sense of rightness, of destiny to it.

He pulled back from that thought. It was all wrong, he chided himself. He was the sheriff. He knew nothing of her other than she was injured and needed assistance.

Striding back into the bathroom, he released the water

from the tub and wiped up the floor with several towels. Looking down at his wet shirt, he stripped it off, tossing it on the pile of wet towels.

Exiting the bathroom, he stepped into his walk-in closet, and pulled another flannel shirt from the hanger. He remained in the closet while doing up the shirt then a few minutes more just pacing back and forth in the small space. Finally, not able to put it off any longer, he stepped out.

The woman was face down on his bed. Her shirt had been removed, and the blanket pulled most of the way up her back. JT couldn't quite see what Doc worked on, but Maggie made an amazingly well tuned assistant.

He wasn't surprised. He didn't think there was anything that Maggie couldn't handle. She was of true pioneer stock. A no-nonsense woman who got things done and was there when needed, just like she had been there when he was eight years old, and his mother died. She'd been there again six years ago for a hurt man and a lonely three year old boy, when their wife and mother decided that the big city had more appeal than her husband, child and returning to the small town they'd come from.

Marcy had never been much of a wife and mother. She'd always been so wrapped up in the pretense of social life, and at one time, JT'd been good for it. Tall, handsome, he'd been the captain of the football team, and dreamed of being the best the FBI had. It looked like he had made it when he'd been assigned to Washington, D.C. not long after graduation. He was an up-and-comer, people knew him. Marcy had loved it.

He never realized how wrapped up in the prestige of the place Marcy had become. Not until she had gotten pregnant, then it all came out. She made it no secret it was an accident, a mistake she didn't want. Marcy also didn't want a life with him either.

JT still felt lucky she had told him about the baby, and he was able to talk her out of an abortion. Now he had

Tyler. It surprised him to realize Marcy's desertion no longer hurt him quite so much.

Looking to the bed, he felt another surge of panic at the sight of a woman in it. Six years ago Marcy's betrayal had killed any desire to have a woman there or, at least, the wish to give into the desire. This woman didn't count, he told himself again firmly. She was a victim, part of his job, but as he looked down at her creamy shoulder where Doc worked, he felt awareness stir within him. He studied her gentle features. She was still pretty, even after what she'd been through.

"JT, you might want to look at this," Doc spoke up pulling his attention.

"Something wrong?" He stepped to the bed.

"I'd say we have a real mystery lady here," Doc answered enigmatically.

"What do you mean?" JT leaned forward over Doc's shoulder.

"See here." Doc reached up and brushed the hair back from her forehead revealing a bandage. "We have a bump here that split the skin. I put two stitches in it. I would say she did it in the accident, and there's swelling starting in her right wrist. I'm pretty sure that it's just a sprain, and it also is probably from the accident. But see here, her palms." Reaching over, Doc tilted her left palm up to reveal scrapes on it. "The other hand and both her knees are the same."

"So she fell coming here."

"Except, with so much snow out there, the gravel wouldn't have dug into her skin like that, especially through her pants into her knees. Then we have here."

He lowered down the blanket corner to show her shoulder. Six black stitches stood stark against the creamy, smooth skin.

"I took a chunk of wood from that cut. It was impaled into her body like it had been stabbed or shot. Notice the swelling and inflammation. By the looks of the area before I cleaned it, I would say the bleeding stopped and started a couple times, and it's at least several hours old, probably closer to eight maybe ten."

Sliding the blanket down a little further the doctor revealed another set of stitches. "This was another piece of wood, and here ..." He pushed the blanket aside to show a thigh which was marred by two more angry looking slashes. "I still need to do these. This one is a piece of glass, but they look similar. And, they didn't come from that car accident."

For a moment, JT lost himself in his own thoughts. "Anything else?"

"There are several bruises. The largest one covers most of the side of her other hip. I'd say it's a good thing she's unconscious because, even with locals, she'd be pretty uncomfortable. The best thing is I can't see any signs of serious damage or internal bleeding. The biggest concern is concussion with that knot on her head, but her eyes are reactive. It would be more dangerous, with the weather, to try to get her to the hospital or clinic for an x-ray than leaving her right here. I can do everything here with Maggie's help, except for x-raying her wrist and skull. We'll just have to take turns keeping an eye on her for any signs of trouble."

"All right, so we leave her here. I'm going to call it in. I also want to check and see how things are going with the storm." He paused a moment, looking down at the woman in his bed. Maggie handed Doc a square of cleaning gaze and pair of long nose tweezers-like things, and Doc went to work on the cut on her thigh.

A few minutes later, JT left his den after finding out the county was surviving quite well without him. With all the roads closed and cleared, there wasn't much trouble for anyone to get into. Once again, JT headed for the kitchen to appease his long neglected hunger.

"Dad," his son stood as he entered.

"Hey, Ty," he greeted, going to the fridge.

"Do you want some help?"

"Sure, I was just going to make myself a sandwich." JT pulled the meat, cheese and spread out of the fridge while Tyler got out the bread. "Will you grab me the milk?"

"Will she be all right?" his son asked, as he pulled the milk jug out of the fridge and moved up beside him.

JT understood immediately that, though Ty tried to hide it, he was feeling helpless. "She'll be fine. There doesn't seem to be any real damage from the cold, which is a blessing. Frostbite's always a big concern. Fortunately, even with the snow and wind, it isn't overly cold out there. At least, not like if it would've been in mid-winter. Though, it probably didn't feel that way to her. She has a few cuts and bruises." *Cuts that were awfully hard to explain.* "But Doc is taking care of those. In a day or two, she'll be as good as new."

JT noticed his son visibly relax, attesting again to the boy's concern. Once more he felt a wave of thanks for his son. His marriage might have been a major disappointment, but he'd never say that because it gave him Tyler.

જgeorge∞

Outside was more gray then black because of the falling snow. JT couldn't say four o'clock in the morning was one of his favorite times of the day. But during his years with the FBI, and after taking the job of sheriff, he had seen quite a few four-in-the-mornings, even in a rural area in Wyoming.

Doc had settled in the guest room. Maggie had turned the watch over to him, after informing him the woman in his bed hadn't made a sound. Well, she might be quiet, but something about her was sure disquieting to him.

JT turned away from the storm going on outside the window to look back at the bed. The glow from the

29

fireplace bathed it with light. The woman's hair had dried into matted locks, but it still caught the light, framing her face with gold.

He wondered what color her eyes were. Blue, he thought, but they hadn't been open long enough for him to be certain. It didn't matter. Tomorrow she would be out of his bed, out of his house and out of his life. Maybe that wasn't the most charitable attitude for a sheriff, but when it came to the woman, it was how he wanted it.

JT turned back to the storm outside. He would do his duty. As soon as she woke up, he'd notify her family. And as soon as the road was plowed out, he'd get her to the hospital, then his duty to her would be done, plain and simple.

A sudden gasp and whimper had him spinning toward the bed. Before he could cross the room, the sounds grew louder and were joined with her tossing and struggling against the blankets. Her movements quickly turned desperate, her breathing hard. Afraid she would hurt herself, JT sat on the edge of the bed and caught her arms.

She cried out then whimpered.

Careful not to hurt her, he locked both her wrists in one hand while he fought to calm her with the other. "Easy, quiet, it's all right," he comforted, softly stroking her face and hair in a manner he'd use with a startled horse. For a moment, she fought harder, then as her strength faded, so did her struggling, allowing his words or the tone of them to seep in. Slowly the whimpering ebbed, and she slipped again into a peaceful sleep.

The peace didn't last long. Almost as soon as he rose, the trembling and whimpered cries returned. She stilled again at his touch. He shrugged it off. *Not his, anyone's.* She didn't know him anymore than he knew her. Still, he sat on the bed with her just as anyone would do for someone who was hurt and plagued with nightmares. Nightmares − that troubled him more on a personal level than he liked to admit.

Sometime before sunrise, he must've drifted off. JT pulled himself out of a very disturbing dream concerning the woman in his bed beside him. The woman was now sleeping peacefully against his thigh.

Cursing silently, he worked his way off the bed. He didn't look back at the woman. She wasn't his. Now, if he could just get her out of his mind. JT headed for the shower to cleanse her away.

Chapter Three

Pain. She gasped as it hit her. Her breath brought in the deep male scent that surrounded her, comforted her, even though it was totally unfamiliar. Glancing around the bedroom, she found nothing familiar there.

It was a warm room, in temperature and atmosphere. Deep tones of hunter, navy and beige accented large furniture of rich wood. A masculine room, but she wasn't afraid.

Trying to shift in the bed brought another burst of pain. There didn't seem to be a single place on her body that didn't hurt.

"You're awake." The young male voice startled her.

She jerked toward the doorway and let out another gasp.

"Hang on and I'll get Dad and Doc Phillips."

She guessed the boy to be nine or ten. She wondered if he should be familiar, and if she should know who "Dad" was, but her mind pulled up nothing. She didn't get time to think about it as heavy footsteps, muffled by thick carpet, approached the room.

The gasp that escaped her this time was for the man who filled the doorway then moved into the room which fit him so well. Tall, broad shoulders, dark brown hair, chiseled features softened by eyes that, even at a distance, she could tell were a soft hazel. Again, her memory pulled up no recollection, but instinct yelled of comfort and safety. She knew, without him coming any closer, it would be his scent that surrounded her in the bed.

At the doorway, another man appeared. This one much older, the remaining hair ringing his head was snowy white. He was at least half a foot shorter than the first man, with heavy laugh lines around his eyes. A good-looking old gentleman, she decided was an apt description of him.

CR80

Blue. Her eyes were blue, the incredible blue of the sky on a perfect day. They also looked very confused as they darted from him to Doc, then back to him. At least her eyes seemed to hold none of the fear that plagued her early morning dreams. They were open wide and alert.

"Hello there." Doc's greeting drew her attention back to him. "How are you feeling?" He moved to the bed.

"Fine," she gave an automatic reply. It changed to a small cry as she shifted in the bed. "I hurt." The declaration was slightly breathless.

"That's understandable. You were pretty banged up."

"What happened?" Her glance flickered over to him, then back to Doc.

"You don't remember?" Doc asked gently.

She made a small shake of her head.

"Why don't you tell me what you do remember?" Doc urged.

The woman closed her eyes and was silent a moment. When she opened them, a tear trickled down her cheek. "Nothing." The answer was whispered so softly JT would have missed it if he hadn't been listening so closely.

"That's all right." Doc settled on the edge of the bed, patting her hand. "It was probably quite a terrifying experience. It's not uncommon for someone to forget an accident. I'm Doctor Phillips, closest neighbor to JT here."

"What happened?"

JT didn't miss the fact that she didn't give her name. He let Doc handle the conversation. "Your car slid off the road in the blizzard last night. Luckily, you made it here before you collapsed."

The woman raised her right hand to her forehead.

"Careful there." Doc caught her wrist as she touched the bandage.

She flinched.

"You got quite a bump and two stitches under the bandage." Doc lowered her hand to her side and patted it. "Don't worry though, they're close enough into the hair line no one will ever notice the scar."

"What else happened?" She looked at her left wrist.

"I'm pretty sure you just sprained that. We'll have to wait for the snow to stop, and the roads to be cleared before we can get you to the hospital to have it X-rayed. Other than that, mostly scrapes and bruises to go along with about a dozen and a half other stitches on your body. I promise nothing serious."

"Was anyone else hurt?" Her expressive eyes seemed to plead for a negative answer.

"No. I checked your car and didn't see another soul."

She let out the breath she'd been holding. "Thank you." Her voice was back to a whisper.

JT decided it was time for some information. He stepped to the end of the bed, drawing her attention. "What's your name?"

Under close scrutiny, he saw her chin tremble. "You don't know me?" She looked expectant at each of them.

He felt a growing unease as she watched both him and Doc shake their heads. The quiver in her chin became more prominent. After a moment of quiet, she finally spoke again. JT felt the words coming but didn't want to hear them.

"I don't know … my name." The words on the end squeaked out as she fought not to cry.

Immediately, Doc squeezed her hand reassuringly, but it was him that her eyes focused on, the watery blue of them digging straight to his soul.

"Please." This time the whisper couldn't be heard, but it roared through his mind just like it did when he first opened the door to her.

After another twenty minutes of no answers, they let her plead exhaustion. She was asleep before both men left the room.

ᏣᏍᏞᎤ

"What do you think?" JT asked.

"If you mean, is she faking it. No. Without X-rays, I can't say if it's due to swelling in the brain. Though honestly, there doesn't seem to be any of the other signs you'd look for. I'd say it's probably trauma-related. In all probability, her memory could be back the next time she wakes up. If it isn't, the odds are that it'll come back soon. Most amnesia cases are not long-term."

JT nodded thoughtfully. "All right. In the meantime, I'm going to take a snowmobile and go check out her car. See if I can come up with some information."

ᏣᏍᏞᎤ

When Jana woke again, the answers were still not there, but the feeling of confusion wasn't quite so strong. She was alone in the room and was comforted by the glow of the fire and scent of the man in whose bed she slept. The picture she pulled up of him in her mind was clear and precise down to the very slight cleft in his chin.

JT. She didn't even know what the letters stood for or for that matter, what his last name was. What she did have was a strong sense of peace. A comfort she didn't understand and, somehow, knew she'd never had before.

"You're awake again." She was pulled from the thought as a woman, she guessed was in her early sixties, came bustling into the room carrying a tray. "When I checked earlier, you were still sleeping. I was asleep the first time you woke. My name is Maggie Price. I'm JT's aunt. If you need anything, just let me know. I have a little breakfast for you to eat."

Maggie placed the tray over her then reached out automatically and arranged her hair over the bandage. "Do you remember anything yet?" Compassion filled the woman's voice.

At the shake of her head, Maggie carried on.

"Well, right now, they have you listed as Jane Doe; procedure and all. If you can think of another name ..." she let it hang.

Jane didn't sound right. Then again, no other name that ran through her mind sounded right either. Shrugging her shoulders, she replied. "I guess Jane's fine. What did the doctor say?"

"Time. He'll be in here soon to check on you."

"He's still here?"

"Until the snow lets up and the plows get here. Don't worry. We'll be one of the first plowed out so they can get JT. He took one of the snowmobiles to your car, so we should have a name for you soon. He'll also make sure it's out of the way or at least marked so the snowplow won't hit it. You're not eating."

"I'd ... I'd like to wash up first, please, if that's okay?" Jana felt a wave of self-consciousness run through her.

"Of course, you better let me help you." Maggie moved the tray out of the way so Jana could swing her legs off the bed. Her first effort to stand wasn't very successful, having to sit back down when the room began to spin.

"Easy there, wait for my help." Maggie caught her arm.

It took them over a minute and a half to cover the fourteen feet to the bathroom. Once Jana had a firm grip on the cabinet and assured Maggie she was all right, Maggie left her on her own.

The image in the mirror shocked her. The blue eyes and light brown hair were unfamiliar to her. She could've been looking out the window at a stranger, instead of a mirror. Plenty of her body was on display in the T-shirt that she guessed was JT's.

The shiver that ran through her was more excitement than cold. She pushed the silliness away and continued to study herself. Her face wasn't a bad face. Not gorgeous, but pretty enough. She guessed you could say average. Maybe if her hair wasn't such a mess, it would help.

Her legs were pretty good, even if she said so herself. There was a bandage on one thigh. Her knees were scraped. Her body was on the lean side, definitely not voluptuous, but shapely enough. No tummy bulge. She wondered how old she was. Twenties, she guessed.

She washed her hands and face, and then unable to resist the comb that lay on the counter, she picked it up and started to work it through her hair. Once finished, she felt much better, but wished she had a toothbrush. The knock on the door startled her.

"How are you doing in there?" Maggie's voice came from the outside.

"Fine." She opened the door. Her legs were not as shaky as they'd been before. She was halfway to the bed when she realized there was another person in the room. She spun toward the doorway where JT stood.

"Oh." Jana wavered as the motion made her dizzy. When her head cleared, she found herself trapped against a hard male body by one strong arm. "Oh," she exclaimed again looking up to his face. Heat crept up her cheeks as she realized all she had on was a thin T-shirt – his T-shirt.

She felt a wave of embarrassment. Unable to keep meeting his look, she dropped her head, but when she tried to step back, he held her tight. Bending slightly, he slid his other arm behind her legs and scooped her up as if she weighed nothing.

"We'd better get you back to bed. You shouldn't be up."

"Maggie helped me," was all she could think to say as he lowered her to the bed. She quickly pulled the blankets up over her body. "Thank you." She didn't meet his eyes but concentrated on her fingers fidgeting with the covers.

CB&O

JT stepped back. The woman was blushing. And not just a little for fake modesty, but a full-blown true one that ran all the way down under the collar of her shirt, correction, his shirt. He forced his eyes away but it was hard. The only women he knew that still blushed were a few of the older women in town that twittered with it.

"You're welcome," he said brusquely, not liking his reaction to her body and those incredible legs. He'd noticed they were decent before. Okay, they were good, but now they were … incredible. He had to bite back a groan he didn't appreciate.

"Maggie said that you had gone to my car." She still didn't look at him. "You know my name now?"

"I'm afraid no such luck."

Her head came up with a jerk.

"The car is registered to a corporation, and I couldn't find your purse. You probably had it with you and dropped it. It's most likely buried in the snow somewhere. I did find your overnight bag. There was no identification on it or any of its contents. No prescriptions or such either. There wasn't a suitcase. I searched the car pretty thoroughly."

Her head dropped in defeat, and though she was not looking at him, he could see her chin quiver.

"Don't worry. I'll run a check on the car. We'll find out who you are."

"You can do that?" She looked up with watery eyes.

"Sure, once I get into the office."

"Office, you're a policeman?"

"Well, sheriff actually, we're rural out here."

"So you can find me?" Hope filled her words.

"Sure. We can't leave you as Jane Doe." He wanted to kick himself for the way her chin quivered again at his comment. "Don't worry about it. It shouldn't be long.

Someone will be looking for you."

She nodded in reply, biting the edge of her lip.

"Maggie left you some breakfast. Why don't you try eating a bite? She'll be back in a minute. You don't want to hear it if you haven't made a sizable dent in that food."

He made it to the door when the voice came from behind him. "Umm, excuse me … but I don't even know your name either."

He turned back. "JT Termaine," he said abruptly, not liking what the soft voice was doing to him.

"JT?" He could see her question but didn't want to answer. Even knowing it wasn't very charitable of him, he didn't want the woman in his life any more than she already was. And that went along with her knowing his full name. But, looking back at those big eyes of hers, they seemed to say, she needed to know and he found himself complying, "Jackson Thomas."

"Jackson Thomas Termaine." She put together. "Thank you, Sheriff Termaine."

♋

"Hi!"

"Hi." She looked up, greeting the boy that stood in the doorway.

"I brought you a glass of milk and a couple cookies. Aunt Maggie said I could."

"Thanks."

He approached, holding a tray with only one glass on it.

"You're not going to join me?" Jana let the touch of loneliness come through.

"I'm not supposed to disturb you."

"I would really like the company." She watched him shift back and forth, obviously eager to join her. "I'll wait while you get another glass."

That was all it took. "I'll be right back."

She smiled, feeling warm inside. What a great kid. He

was such a cute boy, tall and lean, with the same hazel eyes and brown hair as his father. Father! He was JT's son. If he had a son, where was his wife?

A shiver of ice ran through her. She had just been lusting after a married man. Even if she hadn't been going to do anything about it, it was bad.

"Back." The boy was so enthused, she couldn't help smile again. He settled on the bed without hesitation or sign of shyness.

"Well, tell me your name?"

"Tyler, Aunt Maggie and Dr. Phillips said you don't remember yours."

She shook her head.

"That sounds funny forgetting your own name and stuff. What's it like?"

The question was asked so honestly that was how she answered. "Scary, I'm really frightened." For a minute she was afraid she would start to cry.

"Don't be. Dad will take care of you. He used to be with the FBI before he became sheriff. He's really good." There was an unwavering confidence in the words.

JT Termaine was so lucky to have a son who obviously still thought of him as his hero. Jana felt a sense of warmth fill her. "You can't get a better recommendation than that," she agreed, biting into a cookie.

Tyler nodded, his mouth full.

"I haven't met your mom yet."

"She doesn't live here. She's in Washington D.C. She didn't want to come back to the ranch." This time the words were matter-of-fact.

"You must miss her."

"Naw, I really don't remember much about her. She and dad were divorced by the time I was four. I don't visit anymore. She's remarried and lives in a big house where I always have to be careful what I touch. And her husband, Raymond, I don't think he likes kids."

She didn't miss the fact he didn't say anything about his mother visiting him, but how could a mother stay away from such a wonderful child?

"Aunt Maggie takes care of us. Actually, she's my dad's aunt. That makes her my great-aunt, but it's just Aunt Maggie. Her husband died a long time ago. They didn't have any children. She moved back here when we did. This was my grandpa's ranch and his father's before him. Their family was some of the first settlers in the area. My great-grandpa was also the sheriff."

In the next ten minutes, she learned more about the family than she figured his father would want her knowing. JT managed about a hundred head of beef and thirty horses. It was the horses he loved most. They had a ranch hand, Seth, who was an old retired rodeo cowboy. He'd been on the ranch since before Tyler was born. He was seventy-three years old with a limp but could still do anything with a horse. "He's almost as good as Dad."

"Tyler," Maggie entered the room. "Don't you think it's about time you let her get some rest." There wasn't much admonishment in her tone. Still the young Termaine looked over, evaluating her. "Yeah," he concluded.

"Why don't you head out to help your father shovel snow?" Maggie said.

"All right, see you later." He slid off the bed.

"Bye Tyler. Thanks for keeping me company."

He smiled back and headed out the door.

"Hope he didn't bother you too much," the woman asked concerned.

"Not at all. He's a wonderful boy. Maybe someday …" A strong yearning filled her. "Maggie! I don't have children."

"You remember?"

"No." She paused. "Not really remembered. It was more like felt. A wish, a longing, but it was so strong it couldn't have been fulfilled yet. It's still a dream."

"Well, that's a start. You can dream some more now. Get some rest. The plow should be here in an hour or so."

❧

JT slammed the drawer of his desk. He didn't want to think of the woman. He had gotten her out of his house the minute the snowplow cleared the way. She was now at the hospital and out of his hair. Or at least, she would be as soon as the phone lines were back working. Then, he'd get her registration out, and the information about her back. Jane Doe would have a name. Someone would come for her. She would be out of his life for good.

Now if he could just get rid of the feel of her body against his. He pushed the chair back from the desk and paced the small gray office, fighting back the string of curses that wanted to slip out. He'd been trying to teach Tyler that a gentleman didn't swear, but at the moment, he didn't feel much like a gentleman.

What he was feeling was the memory of every slight curve of the woman he wanted to ignore. But her curves had been perfect for him, letting her fit against him in the most intriguing way. And if that wasn't enough, he could still see those big, innocent eyes staring up at him, but he learned a long time ago what was behind innocent eyes, and he wasn't going there again. He liked his life just fine the way it was.

Chapter Four

Jane Doe sat in the hospital room all by herself, wishing she were back in the large comfortable bed that carried JT's scent. She tried to tell herself the thought was inappropriate, but she couldn't help it. Tears crept into her eyes. At JT's, she hadn't felt as alone and scared as she did in this antiseptic-clean room.

She had been poked and X-rayed. Her wrist had a bad sprain and sported a brace, instead of the stretch wrap Dr. Phillips had first put on it. There was no sign of a skull fracture or swelling in her brain.

Dr. Phillips explained to her that he figured her amnesia was trauma-induced, or hysterical amnesia since everything showed clear, and there was no sign of drugs in her system. There was no treatment, but it was possible she could start remembering at any time. He also said it could come back all at once or in bits and pieces.

Now the big question was what was going to happen to her until her memory came back or they found out who she was. There was no physical reason to keep her in the hospital. They only found fifty-five dollars on her, which wasn't enough to pay for a hotel for one night.

She didn't know what she was going to do. There was no way to get a job with no name, no identification, and no skills that she could remember. She had nothing. She shivered, rolling to the side, pushing her face in the pillows to cover the tears.

ଔଏ

JT stopped outside the hospital room. He could hear the muffled sobs from within. He tried to harden his heart against the tortured sound, willing it not to affect him. He might as well have been willing the earth to stop turning.

When he couldn't stand it any longer, he pushed open the door. "Good evening." He tried to make the greeting as casual as possible.

The face that jerked up showed the effects of her crying. Her eyes were red and puffy. Tear streaks on her cheeks. Her chin quivered.

"Problems?" He came and sat in the chair by the bed.

"Do ... you ... know who I am?" The woman sniffled.

"I'm afraid not," he said, trying to soften the news. Tears again slipped down her cheeks, though JT could see her efforts to hold them back.

"What am I going to do? I can't stay here. I don't know what my insurance is or if I have any. I don't have money to cover the bill. I can't get a job. I don't even know what I do. I don't have a name or social security number."

Her worries about insurance and a social security number surprised him. He listed it with the facts that he'd picked up so far. Both worrying about the number and paying the bill suggested she was an honest, conscientious person. He filed the information away in his brain and was reminded of another trait, her fiery blush that had him burning.

"JT." His name being said jerked his attention from the direction his thoughts were going. "I didn't know you were here." Maggie stepped into the room with Dr. Phillips.

"Any news on our young lady?" Doc asked.

"Afraid not. The phone lines are down. Ralph's been after the main office to change that junction for years, and it looks like it finally went out. He said it could take a couple days before it's fixed. Tomorrow, if things are settled down, I'll send Monty to the next town and have it run there. Hopefully, we can get some answers then."

Maggie must have heard the woman in the bed sniffle because she rounded the bed. "There now, there's nothing to worry about. It just might take another day to find out who you are. But we'll be taking you home now anyway."

JT almost jumped out of his seat.

"Home?" The woman in the bed sounded surprised.

"Certainly, they have no reason to keep you here, and I really doubt you want to stay. No offense." Maggie turned to Dr. Phillips then back to the woman. "You would be much more comfortable at the house."

"But," she looked at Maggie then to JT, as if looking for approval.

He didn't even realize he'd nodded until tears sprung to her eyes.

She whispered a soft, "Thank you."

If she knew he really didn't want her at his house, she apparently was too relieved to decline. There was nowhere else she could go.

A few minutes later, JT paced the hall while Maggie helped Jane Doe change back into his T-shirt, robe, and socks which she had worn to the hospital. The outfit should have been ludicrous, but he found it oddly appealing.

Why had he agreed to take her home? He had the opportunity to have her out of his life. At least she would be out of his bed, he consoled himself.

She would be settled in the guest room at the other end of the hall. Not nearly far enough away. It wasn't proper. What was Maggie thinking? He was a single man.

JT shook his head. He knew what Maggie was thinking. It was the right thing to do. She was in need of help. They couldn't just put her in a hotel. She needed looking after. Besides, the hotels were all full with stranded motorists. He'd already checked. There was really no need to worry. Between work at the Sheriff's Office and work on the ranch, he'd be so busy he'd hardly ever see her.

Doc came down the hall with a wheelchair. "Trouble?"

"Just thinking." JT looked up at the man.

"About our missy?" Doc guessed.

"Kind of. I was just wondering about taking her home. I mean, how will it look? I'm a single man."

"Not for the lack of trying by the women in these parts. I wouldn't worry about talk. There's not a person here that doesn't know what a mother hen Maggie is. That woman has an inexhaustible supply of love, and enough sass and spirit to make us all jump. Your honor will be safe under her watchful eye." Doc chuckled.

The door opened before JT could make a comeback.

"Awe, here's our ladies. Missy, if you'll just take a seat," Doc directed.

"I can walk. I'm not dizzy anymore," she protested.

"That's good, but though we're just a small hospital, we still have to follow procedures."

"Which means I have to ride," she finished for him. Her movements were stiff as she settled into the chair.

"You've got it."

The nurse approached them carrying a clipboard. "I have the release papers to sign." The nurse held it out.

She took the board. After staring at it a moment, she looked up. "What do I do?"

"Sign it," the nurse said simply. "It's a release and an agreement to pay when possible."

"But what do I write?" Jana looked around helplessly.

JT noticed a tear escape down her cheek.

Doc must have noticed it too, because he answered, "Jane Doe is fine."

She nodded, taking the pen. The J curved gracefully with a slight open exaggeration, followed by an A then N, but when she got to the E, instead of swooping up and around, she curved back around naturally into an A.

"That's not Jane." The nurse, who had been watching carefully, pointed out.

Jana stared at the name. "Not plain Jane." Her voice

was just above a whisper.

"What was that?" JT knelt down beside her.

Slowly, she brought her large expressive eyes up to look at him. "Not plain Jane. Jana, my name is Jana." She beamed with pleasure.

"Nice to meet you, Jana." He wasn't sure why he said it, but when her smile broke into a little laugh, he was glad he did.

"Last name?" the nurse asked.

Slowly the smile disappeared from her face. She shook her head. "I don't know." Her voice was back to a whisper.

JT immediately missed her smile. "Hey, it's all right." He laid his hand on her arm. "You remembered your first name. That's a start."

The smile returned, though not as bright. Jana nodded. She had to ask the date to finish signing the papers.

JT waited until warm air started to fill the vehicle before pulling up in front of the lobby where the others waited. He got out, bringing with him the quilt they'd used to wrap around Jana when they brought her in.

Jana was much steadier when she stood, though she was still slightly pale, and there were dark circles under her eyes. Stepping to the group, JT dropped the blanket around her shoulders. Without warning, he wrapped an arm around her, sliding the other arm behind her knees, and scooped her up.

He gave little time to voice an objection before he placed her in the front seat of the four-wheel drive vehicle. He tucked the blanket around her body, then closed the door without a word and turned to open the back door for his Aunt.

"No, thanks. I'm going to ride back with Doc." She moved to where the doctor pulled his truck to the curb. "See you at home." She waved merrily as Doc came around the truck to let her in.

JT had to fight the urge to call his aunt back, but what

was he going to say. That the woman disturbed him? He didn't want to be left alone with her? His aunt would sure give it to him for that. He'd never hear the end of it. Helplessly, he went around and got in.

It was a quiet drive as they made their way out of town. JT had just started to wonder if she had fallen asleep when Jana leaned forward, straining to see out the window.

"Is there anything wrong?" he asked.

"Oh, no, just looking at the sky. I can't remember ever seeing so many stars. It's beautiful."

JT didn't answer though he did look out. With the storm moved on, the cold crisp air did make the stars stand out spectacularly.

"It's hard to believe there was a blizzard yesterday. Do nights around here look like this often?"

"Pretty much so. A lot of people think it's a barren area, but if you look, there's a lot of beauty." He found himself answering.

"Well, this is one of the most beautiful nights I've ever seen."

"Could be you're just happy to be alive," he suggested.

"Or remembering, you mean," she filled in, and then shook her head. "No. This is one beautiful night. I know it."

"What do you think the nights are like where you are from?" He glanced her way, wondering if he could jog some memories. He saw the deep thought mar her brow.

"I think the nights are nice, but not so bright, clear, sharp and fresh like this."

JT looked out at the sky. He often looked out and appreciated it. It was one of the things he'd missed most when he lived in D.C. and Virginia. It was one of the reasons that prompted him to give up the choice position he had landed.

His ex-wife had thought he was foolish, but he'd found what was really important to him. He hadn't given up a single thing walking away. Not even his wife, because, by then, she had already gone. No, he hadn't given up anything, he'd been trying to set up the perfect dream, but it had been a fractured lie. Now, when he looked back, he knew what he'd wanted most in life hadn't ever been there.

But, his life was back on track now. He was honest enough to admit something was missing. He just wasn't willing to risk what he had to try and find it. Turning to his ranch, JT smiled contently at the scene. Life felt good.

"Wait here," he instructed, pulling to a stop. He got out and came around to open the door.

"I can walk," she protested when he slid his arms around her.

"And get my socks wet?" He lifted her from the seat. She stiffened when her body pressed against his. "Just relax and put your arms around my neck."

Her arm slid timidly up, turning her body into him. Her hair brushed his cheek. Every muscle in his body tightened in response. His attention focused on the woman in his arms. It was all he could do not to turn her to him more fully, and press his face into the soft waves of her hair.

He was saved when Doctor Phillips pulled in beside them. He got out and rushed to get the door open, but Tyler beat him to it holding the door open for everyone to come in.

"You're back," he sounded excited to see Jana.

"They didn't know what else to do with me. The only other option was to let your father arrest me for loitering and indecent exposure and throw me in jail," she kidded.

"Yeah, we're tough on vagrants around here. I think the sentence is a good meal and being sent to bed. It smells wonderful in here." JT found himself picking up the teasing.

"Aunt Maggie started a stew earlier, but I have the table all set."

"Great, let's eat then." JT headed to the kitchen table

with her still in his arms.

"I think you can put me down now," Jana whispered.

"We're already about there." His chest tightened as her breath tickled his ear. Lowering her to the floor, his arms felt strangely empty. He had the urge to pull her back in.

"I'd better wash up," he said, still looking down at her.

Her face turned to his. Her eyes widened, giving her a slightly confused look. Jana's bottom lip caught between her teeth. She nodded mutely.

Jana took a deep breath as he walked away. She felt strangely lightheaded and this time doubted it had anything to do with the blow to her head. JT Termaine packed a wallop. She shook the thought off. She just needed some food and sleep, but her eyes followed the man who took her breath away just by how he moved in that confidant fluid way.

"You're going to stay here a couple days?" Ty chirped up, and she turned to him.

"It looks like it. At least until we can figure out who I am. By the way, my name is Jana."

"You got your memory back," he exclaimed excitedly.

"No, just my first name." She tried to not sound disheartened.

"That's still cool though."

"Yeah," she smiled, a wave of confidence blossomed within her. "It is."

After eating, Jana got settled in the guest bedroom. Not that she had much to move in. Her overnight bag held the basic hair care products, personal items and a small amount of makeup, which hinted that she normally didn't wear much.

There was also a small jewelry bag which held nothing big or showy but a few nice necklaces, a couple bracelets and an assortment of earrings, most of which were posts or small dangles. She figured it said a lot about her personality. She might not be a plain Jane, but she wasn't a flashy woman either.

Jana sighed, sitting back on the bed. She liked the room. It had a more feminine feel than JT's room, with antiques and a pieced quilt. She figured it fit her taste very well but she missed the warm comfort of JT's.

She lay back, pulling the blankets up around her, missing the musky smell of JT on the pillows. Still, it was better being here than in the hospital. Here there was a secure feeling, like a balm she didn't quite understand but could appreciate. Closing her eyes, she drifted to sleep.

掐掀

JT went through the house turning off the lights and locking up, a habit left over from living in the city. As sheriff, he knew you still had to be careful even in a small rural community.

At the doorway to Tyler's room, he stopped a moment and watched his son sleep before crossing the floor. He ran his finger over the hair that was so near the color of his own. It was a nightly habit that started when his son was a baby and his hair downy soft. He felt the usual surge of love and pride. He had a great son.

In the hall, he paused outside the guest room, trying to push away the thoughts of the woman within. He'd intended on heading down the hall, but as if it had a will of its own, his hand caught hold of the knob. He pushed open the door just enough for the light to spill onto the bed and the woman that slept there. A soft innocence shrouded her. JT wondered if it was due to her lack of memories, or if she always had this quiet compelling quality about her. Not giving himself time to think about it, he shut the door.

A few minutes later he sighed, lying back in his bed. Sleep didn't come. A feeling of emptiness filled him along with the faint lingering feminine smell that the clean sheets on his bed didn't purge. Cursing the woman who'd invaded his life, he rolled over and tried to force his thoughts from her.

CR8O

Sun warmed the room when Jana woke and stretched the next morning. A steady dripping sound came from melting snow running off the roof. As a child, she used to love bright days after the storm when the sunlight glistened off the snow, melting it away. No sooner had she thought about it, the memory was gone, leaving her with just a fleeting glimpse of lavender walls and unicorns.

Feeling slightly discouraged, she slid from under the covers. Her muscles protested, more sore than they had been the previous day. Carefully, she made it to her feet and across the hall into the bathroom.

The sight that greeted her wasn't any better than what her body felt. Her hair hung limp and oily around her face. The bruise that framed the bandage was an array of angry purple, blues, ghastly green, and yellow.

Washing her face made the scrapes on her hands sting. At least she had a toothbrush. She looked longingly in the mirror at the shower before deciding she'd better wait, and make sure Tyler was ready for school before she tied up the bathroom that long.

Maggie was washing dishes when she entered the kitchen.

"Good morning." The woman turned when she heard her.

"Good morning."

"How are you feeling today?"

"Sore," Jana answered truthfully.

"Well, let's get you some breakfast, then you can have a hot shower to help relieve some of those aches. I'll also change your bandages and see if I can find you something else to wear."

The breakfast was wonderful, but the shower was heavenly. It made her feel almost normal to be dressed again and moving around the house, helping and talking with Maggie.

ങ്ങൃ

JT was exhausted when he walked into the house. Morning hadn't even started when he was called to the next town to handle a domestic dispute, drunk and disorderly. Not a great way to start the day.

Monty had called in sick, leaving him short-handed. And, Mrs. Murray's cow got in Edith Hemming's yard. The two women got into such an argument that there was a fender bender caused by people trying to watch what was happening.

He thought the two women were going to come to blows before he finally got them settled down. After that, he endured an hour of listening to years' worth of complaints from lifetime rivals. He was glad he wasn't the one who was going to judge the jams and preserves at the fair this year because, if either woman won, it was going to be a war.

The house was quiet, so he followed his nose to the kitchen. At the door he froze, his eyes locked on the taunt denim-clad rear that swayed teasingly back and forth to some inner music. Trim legs stretched a generous way down to once-white tennis shoes, but his eyes returned to the tantalizing bottom as the rest of Jana's body was bent over the table.

Reaction hit, and hit him hard, yelling to him he was still alive and had desires long neglected.

"Great." The soft voice he'd come to associate with his houseguest sounded enthused, and the figure straightened.

"Dad." Tyler saw him from where he was sitting at the table. "I just finished my math. Jana's a whiz at numbers."

The woman who turned to him looked nothing like the one who had wandered in out of the storm. The shoes were hers, but the jeans, if he didn't miss his guess, were a pair of his that had accidentally gotten washed in hot water and shrunk. He'd intended to give them away a long time ago. Now, he was glad he hadn't. Despite the fact that the jeans were rolled up a good six inches, he thought they had never looked like that on him.

The navy sweater she wore was one that Tyler's mother had sent him. It was a few sizes too large for Tyler and cashmere. Beautiful, but Ty would never wear it, even when he grew big enough to fit it, and it sure wouldn't look like that on Ty. Jana had pushed the sleeves up to almost her elbows. The shoulders fit nicely. The waist bagged a little, but the soft knit hugged lovingly across her breasts. Not voluptuous but full curves. Nice, very nice.

The hair that had been a dirty, stringy mass of disarray was now washed clean and hung in soft, glistening, wheat-colored locks that feathered around her shoulders. Her face showed little signs of makeup.

He became aware she was studying him with those incredible blue eyes. He struggled to steer his thoughts to a safe area.

"More memories?" Thankfully, his voice sounded only slightly gruff.

She shook her head. "No, though I discovered that I like math."

"She's fast, Dad. Beats me with a calculator. I bet even faster than Mrs. Reynolds on the times tables."

"Sounds good."

Jana shifted, color pinked her cheeks. Her chin dropped but not before he saw a slight smile tip up her lips. She was blushing again, actually blushing.

"You're looking pretty good." That was an understatement he made no effort to correct.

"These are a pair of your jeans, I hope you don't mind?" Her eyes came up to him, though her chin only raised a little. It was a perfect flirt movement, but JT figured she hadn't calculated it as such. The woman had a shy side. He wondered if it would still be there when her memories returned.

"Not at all," he answered, forcing his attention to what

they had been saying.

"Tyler let me borrow one of his sweaters."

"Actually, I gave it to her." Tyler confirmed what JT had guessed.

"You might want it back," she insisted.

Ty gave her a look that was dubious at best. There was nowhere around here for a boy Tyler's age to wear anything quite like that and not feel like a sissy. Not that Tyler wouldn't dress up; he would for church and when needed. But the sweater was not Tyler. It was perfect for Jana, though.

JT found he wanted to slide his arm around the soft knit and run his hands over it, and feel the soft womanly curves against him. This obsession was getting out of control.

"Do I smell dinner?" JT changed the subject to a safer area.

"Oh, I'll get it, if you want to wash up." Jana moved to the stove.

JT stepped to the sink. "Where's Maggie?"

"She went to take something to Doctor Phillips. We ate earlier."

"That's fine, I got held up." He went on to regale them with tales of wandering cows and disputing old ladies. "Jana, I'm sorry but I wasn't able to send Monty to run the check today. They assured me the phone lines would be up tomorrow, though. I'll run your registration first thing."

She nodded and forced a slight smile out. "Can I get you anything else?" She placed a plate in front of him.

"I'm fine."

"You have apple pie for dessert. Would you like ice cream with it?"

"I think you could talk me into it."

"You mean if I warm the pie first?" She now grinned.

"Well, we know one more thing."

"What's that?"

"You're a good woman."

Jana's laughter made things feel a little too warm, too comfortable, and too intimate. Even with his son there – especially with Ty there. It felt like a family, but that was an illusion. Emotionally, JT pulled back.

The smile disappeared from Jana's face as if she sensed his withdrawal. JT ignored her and turned to Tyler. "How's the homework coming along?"

"Just finished."

"You want to walk down to the stables with me? Seth thinks Cheyenne's going to foal any day now. I want to keep an eye on her. He also left Rosie, Ruthie Bell and Snickers in. They're getting close. So as they say, the race is on."

"Jana, do you want to come?" Tyler asked.

She brightened a minute, then glance from Ty to him.

JT didn't like the thought of her intruding on his and Tyler's time. It must've showed on his face, because she grew somber and shook her head.

"I have had about all I can handle today. I think I'll turn in now. Maybe I can see them tomorrow. Goodnight."

"Night, Jana." Tyler disappeared to get his denim jacket leaving the two adults in the room.

Jana looked away, back, then away again. "I'll just do these dishes."

"Leave them. I'll do them when I get back. You should take it easy on your wrist." He nodded to the brace on her arm.

She looked down at it then turned her hand over to reveal the scrapes. "All right, I'll just head to bed."

JT heard her pass Tyler in the hall. A second later, Ty entered the room ready to go.

From her bedroom, Jana could see out to the stables. She could clearly make out the two figures walking across the yard. JT had his arm draped over his son's shoulder. She wanted to join them, but it was obviously a father and son time, and JT did not want her invading.

The lights were still on when she came from the bath and slipped into JT's large T-shirt. She wondered if the colt would be born tonight. Again, she wished she could go see. Instead, she pulled back the covers, climbed into bed, and drew the blankets up around her. She ignored the images of JT that flashed through her mind as she willed herself to sleep.

CB&O

The house was quiet when Jana exited her room the next morning. Even Maggie wasn't in the kitchen. On her own, she found cereal and a bowl. Even with the cumbersome brace, she managed to wash the dishes that had been left in the sink. She had just finished and was wondering what else she could do when Tyler burst in the back door.

"Jana," he yelled.

"Hi." She stepped into the room. "I thought you were in school."

"I got to take the morning off. Come on." His voice was urgent.

"What is it? Is Maggie hurt?" Alarm bells rang in her head and her heart raced.

"No, Cheyenne's having her colt." He grabbed her hand.

Jana was out the door and running with him without any conscious decision.

Maggie was in the stable along with Seth, the old ex-rodeo cowboy she had met the day before. They nodded a greeting, but all their attention was on the stall.

JT was inside, squatting beside the mare lying on her side. His large hand stroked gently over the horse's swollen stomach as it heaved with its labored breathing.

"Is she all right?" Jana whispered.

Maggie nodded. "She's handling it good. Shouldn't be long now."

As she spoke the mare's side gave a great heave. Jana heard JT whispering to the horse. He comforted the mare with his touch, watching for signs of trouble.

A quarter of an hour had passed when Jana's breath caught along with everyone else's. She didn't release it until a minute later, when the foal slid into the world. Everyone gave their own gasp of pleasure.

"Oh, wow," Tyler echoed.

"Yeah," Jana agreed, hugging his shoulder. "So incredible." Her eyes came up to meet JT's who now stood back, letting the mare get to her new foal. He met her gaze, then his focused dropped to the arm she had around his son's shoulder. Jana let her arm drop, shifting to the side, suddenly feeling uncomfortable.

⊂�⊃

That woman, she had to be here at this time. The birth of a new colt was a special time to him. And she looked as if it was a special time to her. Then she hugged his son, naturally, as if she didn't even think about it before doing it.

Tyler's mother never touched her son with that ease, even as a baby. Each time Tyler's mother touched him it had been calculated, even forced. JT felt his ire rise and scowled in recognition. A stab of jealousy of his own son followed, deepening his anger, letting it show on his face so that Jana pulled back, stepping away from his son.

His attention shifted as the mare made it to her feet. With little nudges from her nose and after two tries the foal made it up on spindly legs.

"All right everyone. Let's let this little filly and her mama get better acquainted." He started to herd everyone out only to have Jana hang back to catch one last glance of the foal. Unable to help himself, JT touched her arm. Jana's eyes remained on the foal, which nudged eagerly, having found her mother's nipples.

"Isn't that incredible. She's so beautiful."

"Would you like to name her?" The words were out before he realized it.

"Oh, but wouldn't Tyler like to?"

"Who do you think named the last dozen foals we've had?"

A small laugh escaped her. "Can I have some time to think of a good name? I mean, it's not something you want to mess up on. Names are important."

His anger slipped, and he smiled at her attempt to make light of her own situation. "Take all the time you need." Then he stiffened, realizing he'd once again let the woman get under his skin. He turned. "Come on, son." He dropped a hand to Ty's shoulder moving him toward the house.

They had a quick, early lunch then JT took Tyler with him to drop him off at school before going into the office. He was called away immediately, and it was three o'clock when he finally got back in. To his further frustration, the phone lines were still not up, but he was assured it would only be another hour. It was closer to two hours before the line was active.

The check didn't illuminate anything. The registration on the car only listed a company, and the phone number his search revealed wasn't answered. It was near six when he finally gave up. Figuring the business was closed for the day.

Instead of going into the house, he went directly to the stable to check on the newest addition to his ranch. The sound of voices reached him as he stepped to the barn.

"Like horses?" He heard Tyler.

"Yeah, I guess I do, but I don't think I've been riding for a while," the soft female voice answered.

"Maybe I can take you on Saturday."

"I'd like that, but we'd better get busy now if we're going to finish chores before your dad gets home."

"Right, the foal is sure cute, isn't she? Have you come

up with a name yet?"

Jana's laughter filled the air. "It's only been ten minutes since you last asked me."

"Well?"

"Any suggestions?"

"No, but don't name it something stupid like starlight or moonbeam. That's what the girls at school always do." There was disgust in his voice.

Jana laughed again. "I'll take care, no sappy, girly names. My mother's horse was Slippers, but since this one doesn't have socks, I guess that doesn't fit."

"Your mother had a horse?" Ty asked.

"What?"

"You said your mother's horse."

"My mother had a horse." There was hesitancy in the voice. "It was a palomino. I can remember riding her when I was little."

"Remember anything else?"

Quiet filled the stable.

"No, I thought … for an instant, but it's gone." She rubbed her temple.

"Do you have a headache?"

"It just came on. Let's grab the hay. I think we're done here. Oh!" she gasped, coming around the partition, and ran right into JT.

He reached out to steady her.

"Oh," she gasped again, grabbing a hold of him.

"Hi." JT looked down at the startled woman. Her face turned up to him as if in offering. He was about to take possession of her lips when Tyler stepped out.

"Dad, we were just finishing chores."

"I see." JT released Jana. "How are our new little filly and her mama doing tonight?"

"Great, come see."

JT joined his son at the stall. The little fuzzy bronze-colored filly was now steady on her long, knobby-kneed legs. But, to any horsemen, she looked wonderful.

JT opened up the gate and stepped inside. The foal slid behind its mother as JT approached. Cheyenne rubbed her head against his arm as he greeted her.

"How's the mama tonight, huh, girl?" He rubbed her neck. "Did yourself proud, didn't you?" Carefully he held out his hand and gave the curious little foal time to check it out.

He chuckled softly as the little horse spooked itself and frisked around the stall before coming back to him. This time she let him slide his hand over her. After a second, he turned his attention back to the mother, rubbing her neck and saying a few more words to Cheyenne before stepping out of the gate.

"Guess what? Jana had horses when she was young, or at least her mom did. She also knew how to clean out the stall."

"Hope you didn't work her too hard," JT teased.

"We worked together," Tyler said proudly.

"It looks great. What do you say we go in and eat? I'm starved."

Walking close to Jana, he asked quietly. "Any other memories?"

"Just my mother had a palomino named Slippers. Did you find out anything?"

"Afraid not. The car's registered to a corporation. No name on it. I have managed to get a phone number, but no one answers. I'll try again tomorrow."

⋘⋙

Peter Ferrell sauntered through the glass door at twenty to eight in the morning. The huge office was busy, but it was nothing compared to what it would be in another hour.

"Hey, Judy, what's up?"

"Oh, the usual"

"Anything for me?"

"Couple of messages, Tanner wants an update on the

bombing. He wants something to point to Kellerman."

"Don't we all? Any word on Jake?"

"It still doesn't look good."

Ferrell's eyes ran over the desk, looking for anything he might be interested in. What he saw raised more than his interest. With subtle movements and a little sleight of hand, he palmed the memo without Judy being the wiser. With everything the secretary handled, he figured she'd never even notice it missing.

"Well, duty calls. I'd better get to work." He moved through the cubicles to his own. He didn't have to worry about the phone there being tapped or traced.

Quickly he punched the numbers from memory.

"Yeah," was said in way of an answer.

"Got something. A check on the car." Ferrell glanced out into the hallway, making sure it was clear.

"Check from whom?" The tone of worry came through the phone lines.

"A sheriff from a small town in Wyoming, Wilson Butte."

"What's he checking on?"

"Don't know. I don't dare interfere."

"You sure she's still alive?" The voice pressed on the other end of the line.

"Positive. She drove the car away."

"Well, go after her."

"I can't. I'm stuck here, trying to head off the investigation and cover this up. You're going to have to do it yourself. It would do you good to get out of sight for a while. Just don't get trigger happy," Ferrell stressed.

"I paid you to take care of it."

"I will. Just find out if she's there and let me know, and I'll come do your dirty work."

"You think she's still willing to testify?"

"I don't think you can leave it open to chance, do you."

"No, especially not with a sheriff sniffing around."

"So why don't you go check out the sights and keep an eye out for a wayward accountant? If they're in season, I'll be right there for the hunt. I always see my jobs through."

"What's that name again?"

"Wilson Butte, Wyoming."

Chapter Five

JT slammed the phone down. He was getting frustrated. There was no answer still. If Jana was the sole employee, it might make sense, but there should have been an answering machine. Everyone had them.

It also bothered him that he couldn't get any information on the company. All his checking had turned up nothing. If he were more suspicious, he would say it was a dummy corporation for a cover, but that was just too farfetched.

He had to do something and fast. He had almost kissed her last night in the stable. He'd totally forgotten Tyler was in the barn with them. He'd lain awake a good part of the night thinking of how she'd felt up against him, of the soft lips parted in invitation.

She would be sweet, he knew, but wondered if her missing memory would make her awkward, with no experiences to draw from, or would the knowledge remain? He was sick. He liked the thought she would remember no other man's kisses and lovemaking. But, she didn't know who she was and until she did, she wouldn't be his to kiss or anything else. Not that he wanted to be involved with the woman anyway.

He pushed the chair back and stood. He needed a break. Grabbing his hat, he walked out the door. It felt good to walk around town, chatting to people. It helped clear his head.

"JT."

He turned at the sound of his name being called. Ted Call, the owner of the town's newspaper, headed across the street toward him. "Join me at the café," Ted beckoned.

"Could this mean you want to pump me for information?" JT joked back.

"It sure does," Ted returned.

"Lead the way." The two headed down the street.

"I heard about the woman that had an accident," Ted started.

"Figured you did." JT pulled open the café door. Ted didn't speak again until they were seated in the booth.

"What can you tell me?"

Before JT could answer, the waitress came up. After ordering a piece of strawberry-rhubarb pie and a glass of milk, he turned to Ted.

"Well, the gist of it is, our mystery woman slid off the road down by my place. She was lucky she made it to the house. She was half-frozen and a little banged up." JT breezed over her injuries, not mentioning that most happened before her accident. He hadn't come up with an explanation for that, yet.

"Doc was able to get to my house and patch her up," JT continued. "Except for her memory, she's doing fine. We know her first name is Jana, and she was driving a car with Colorado plates. I haven't been able to get any information on it yet. Phone lines being down slowed that process up."

"She's staying at your place?"

"You know Maggie and have to ask?" JT cast a look at him that asked if there was any doubt.

Ted laughed.

"Howdy boys," Noma walked up to the table with their order.

"Haven't seen you for a couple of days," JT greeted the motherly type waitress.

"Caught that silly flu going around. This is my first

time back since the storm. It was nasty."

"Storm or flu?" JT grinned.

"Both." She met his look. "By the way, I've been wondering, did that young lady find you?"

"What lady?"

"The day of the storm a young woman came in. Pretty and really sweet, but she was troubled, kind of jumbled. She sat here so quiet. Then she asked about you and directions to your place. Right after she left, the storm really picked up. I was worried if she made it. I was going to call when I got home, then I ended up sick."

"Your mystery woman?" Ted said what JT was thinking.

"Can you describe her?" JT asked.

"Sure. She had me by a couple inches, so five-seven to five-eight. Real light, brownish-blonde hair that hung just below her shoulders. She had on a man's jacket, but it was a light-weight one, that didn't do much good to keep her warm. She looked so cold."

"Anything else?" JT pressed.

"Let me see, she said her name was," she paused to think. "Jana, that's it. Her name was Jana."

"No last name?

Noma shrugged. "She didn't say, why?"

"You must be slipping if you haven't heard yet? If it's the same woman and I'm positive it is, she had an accident and has amnesia. Noma, can you sit down and tell me everything you remember."

"Sure." Noma waved back to the other waitress then slid into the booth beside him. "It was just starting to snow when she came in. I guess I remember because she looked so lost. And also, when I asked her if she wanted coffee, she told me she didn't drink coffee. She asked for a hot chocolate. I brought her out a new one when she didn't drink her first before it got cold. She had just sat there staring off into space. That's when I asked her if she was all right."

"Did she seem hurt?" JT cut back in.

"Not hurt exactly, but she was a little disheveled. She was definitely troubled, though she said she was fine. But, when I started to walk away, she asked about the police in town. She asked if you were honest."

Noma tilted her head to the side slightly and tapped at finger to her lips. "When I told her you were, she wanted to know where the station was. When I said you wouldn't be there, she wanted to know where your house was. She didn't want to talk to the deputies."

Noma looked right into his eyes. "Understand, I wouldn't have told her how to find you, but she seemed so lost, frightened, and nervous. She was just so worried about who she could trust. You know, I'd say she didn't feel good by the way she moved."

"So maybe she was hurt then," JT thought out loud. "Did she indicate anything else?

"No. That's what made me believe she was frightened. That and the way she asked if you were honest. I hope you don't mind I told her how to find you, but she seemed to need help something fierce."

"I understand. It's okay. Thanks."

"Sure thing, is she still in the hospital? Maybe I'll stop by and see her, a familiar face and all."

"Not a bad idea, but no, she's at my place. You know Maggie. But I'll bring her by later to see if she recognizes anything."

"I'll be here until four tonight."

"All right, see you later."

"Still a mystery," Ted commented.

"Yeah, but at least we have something. I was going to ask you to run her picture, but if someone is after her …" He let the sentence hang.

The newspaper man picked up the line of thought. "It's not likely it's anyone local so you shouldn't have to worry about that. I could just say contact the sheriff's office with any information and not mention where she's staying, though I'm sure half the town knows already. If they don't, they soon will."

"You're right, but try it, leave the information we have on her at a bare minimum." But his instincts kicked in. This could explain some of the questions he had on the pretty young woman. If she was in danger, then she came to the right man, he decided.

"All the information we have is a bare minimum," Ted pointed out.

"True." He turned his attention back to the newspaperman. "But don't put in any of what Noma said about her asking about me. She just had an accident and, for all we know, got the wrong road in the storm. I'll let Noma know not to say anything." He stood to talk to the waitress before leaving.

Back at the office, he had a message waiting about Jana's car. Calling over to Lou's garage, he talked to Lou.

"Got it towed in. The axle looks okay, but it has a hole in the muffler bad enough she could get exhaust fumes in," the mechanic told him. "I wouldn't recommend driving it until it's fixed. It'll be Monday before I get the parts in."

"Thanks," he said to the grizzled old man.

ෆ඀ఠ

"You okay to do that?"

Jana jumped at JT's voice behind her, not hearing him over the vacuum. She turned off the vacuum and nodded, looking at the brace on her hand. "It's not hard doing it one-handed."

He nodded, accepting her answer. "Where's Maggie?"

"Tyler's room, putting away clothes."

"Thanks." He headed down the hall.

Tempted to follow him, Jana instead turned the vacuum back on, going over the floor one more time for good measure. A few minutes later, she looked up to find

JT scowling at her.

In three steps, he closed the distance. His hand slid over hers on the vacuum handle. Finding the switch, he turned it off. The motor became quiet, but the energy continued to run up her arm. She found it impossible to breathe.

"I want to take you to town for a while." His words were tight, as if hard for him to get them out.

"You found something out about me?" She was barely able to keep her voice from squeaking. Jana wondered if he realized he still had her hand trapped under his.

"Not yet. I want to put out a picture in the newspaper, if that's okay."

She nodded though she felt like there was something he wasn't telling her.

"I also wanted to send your fingerprints out to see if they turn up anything," he continued.

"Fingerprints." Jana felt sick. "You think I'm a criminal?"

"No, but it's possible that if you were ever in the military, or most states require teachers and government workers to be printed."

"So it's possible I'm in the data banks."

"Yeah, but I can't force you to be printed. You haven't done anything wrong here." His thumb brushed her knuckles. Her heart jumped, and her throat went oddly dry.

Swallowing, she forced the words out. "It's okay, you can print me." She wondered if she could deny anything Jackson Thomas Termaine wanted. Instinct said, she was totally out of her depth with him.

They fell quiet, their hands still held together. This time she wondered if it was possible that he could be as affected by the surging current as she was, or if he felt anything at all?

She raised her head to look him in the eye. All questions fled her mind as she became trapped in his incredible green-gold eyes. She lost time, lost the world. There were just those eyes, his gentle breaths that caressed her face and the clean musky male scent that permeated her soul. Those eyes dipped closer, coming for her but never breaking contact until they were mere inches away, then abruptly they were gone, leaving Jana no time to figure out what had happened as JT left the room.

A minute later, Maggie entered. "You better take a jacket. There's still a slight chill in the air. JT said he would be waiting for you in the truck."

The ride to town was done in stony silence. Jana wasn't sure what to say. She wondered if she had imagined what had happened, that somehow along with her missing memory, she had lost the ability to judge a situation. She could have sworn JT wanted to kiss her, or maybe it was just that she wanted him to kiss her. She just didn't know what to think, and JT wasn't helping by giving her any clues.

At the newspaper office, JT introduced her to Ted Call, a small balding man who ran the newspaper. Ted took several pictures then promised to have the pictures ready in two hours.

The front area of the sheriff's office was comfortable. JT led her around a long wood counter, past three ordinary office desks, each with a tidy stack of folders on one corner. He paused long enough to introduce her to Alice, the secretary/dispatcher. JT stopped in his office to drop his hat on the old maple desk in his office.

Jana hung back, trying to catch a glimpse of his private workspace. It was more utilitarian than his office at home. Like the rest of the area she had seen so far, it had plain, gray flooring and off-white walls trimmed with dark wood.

A flag stood to one side by a picture of George Washington. There was a window behind his desk, but she was caught by the large painting on the other wall. The mountains were rugged and beautiful with a peaceful lake nestled below. The caption read, "The Wind Rivers".

When she stepped closer to look at the picture, JT moved in behind her. "Those are the mountains you see, on a clear day, in the distance." He turned leaving her to follow. He paused again to introduce her to his deputy, Monty Reeves.

"Ma'am." The man in his early twenties didn't offer his hand. "Sorry, I picked up the cold that's been going around. I don't want to spread it."

"I appreciate that," Jana answered.

"This way." Again JT left her to follow him. He led her to the back of the building. The fingerprinting was set up across from a holding cell. With its old linoleum and its bleak furnishing, the room wasn't nearly as comfortable as the other area had been.

"It's all right," JT encouraged at her hesitation.

Jana managed a nod. She jumped when he took her hand to press her fingers in the ink.

"Sorry, we still have to do this the old fashioned way."

She tried to relax and let him guide her fingers, but his touch seemed to singe her already-stressed senses. When he released her hand and handed her a wipe, she forced a breath into her lungs, only to be rewarded with the smell of the strong cleaner that permeated the area. "Is it always this bad?" She held out her stained hands.

The question seemed to catch him by surprise and he chuckled. "Sorry."

"Yeah, I can tell."

He broke into a full laugh, and handed her another wipe to clean them off. Jana finally felt the tension between them ease. Inwardly, she let out a sigh of relief. She was surprised when JT suggested they walk over to the café.

An older waitress greeted them as soon as they walked in. Jana had the oddest feeling of déjà vu, but she couldn't say why.

"Is something wrong?" JT asked as he settled her in

the exact booth she'd been in before.

"No," Jana shrugged. "Just an odd feeling."

"Like what?"

"Like … I've been here before." She rubbed her temple, trying to pull up the memory.

JT waited for a minute, but when she shook her head, he pressed. "Tell me."

"There's nothing." Her shoulders slumped. "Just a feeling."

"Would you like a hot chocolate today?" Noma's question took her by surprise when the woman came to the table.

"Yes, please." She was shocked. "Have we met before?"

"You were in here the other day."

"Oh."

Noma looked to JT.

"A root beer, please."

After the waitress left, Jana turned to him. "You knew that I'd been here."

"I found out earlier today. I also found out that you bought gas next door, but you used cash so that's a dead end. However, you did tell Noma your name was Jana, so that pretty much confirmed it. Unfortunately, you didn't give her your last name."

"You're not telling me something," she confronted him.

"I was hoping being somewhere you were before the accident would jog your memory."

"JT, please," she pleaded.

He was quiet a minute then sighed. "Noma thought you seemed a little upset or scared. You asked for directions to my place. You were on your way to see me when you went off the road."

Jana fell silent, staring off into space, willing herself to remember. What had happened to her? Why would she need the sheriff so bad that she went out into a storm? Jana wasn't sure what to say as she fought to keep her chin from quivering. Suddenly she felt very much like crying. "You don't know why?" She fought to calm herself.

"No. You didn't say, but I'm gonna find out." He looked at her, making a promise.

She was quiet again when Noma placed their drinks on the table. When she remained that way, JT reached across the table and touched her hand, to bring her attention back to him.

"Don't worry about that now. It could be nothing. So don't go borrowing trouble." He figured it was easier said than done when the only thing you knew was your first name and that you were looking for the Sheriff.

It seemed all she could do was just sip her hot chocolate without crying. JT knew she was still trying to come to terms with the latest obstacle thrown at her. He had to admire how she had handled everything so far, but he really wished he could do something to help her.

"How about we go check on your car? Maybe it will jog something," JT suggested a few minutes later when they stepped out of the café. "Lou's garage is next door. That's where you got gas when you came into town."

She nodded, pulling the jacket she wore a little tighter, though it was nice and warm out.

The gas station brought no memory. She felt extremely hesitant as she followed JT and the old mechanic into the garage bay. The ordinary tan sedan didn't bring anything, but a cold shiver. Jana wondered if it was left over from the accident or being out in the storm.

"I'm sorry I can't get the part in until Monday to fix it," the old man, Lou, apologized.

"It doesn't matter," she assured him. "I don't have a driver's license right now, so I can't drive anyway, and I'm afraid it might be awhile before I can pay for the repairs, but I promise I will as soon as I can."

"Don't worry about that until you're back on your feet, young lady," the grizzled little man with grease strained hands instructed kindly.

"Thank you." Jana smiled. "I promise I'll make good on it," she assured him.

"That's good enough for me," Lou told her, but it didn't ease the heaviness that hit her heart.

"Bye," she said softly, before walking out the open bay door.

JT start to follow her when Lou called him back.

JT watched her go. He hadn't missed the spark of hope that dimmed in her. He wasn't sure how long she could handle the lost, helpless feelings she faced. She had nothing. No money, no identity, no past, no certain future.

"Yeah, Lou." He turned back to the mechanic.

"I wanted to show you this and see what you thought. At first, I didn't think much about it until I noticed this one." He directed the sheriff over to the roof of the car, running his finger next to the crease in the metal.

A jolt of shock ripped through JT, confirming the unease he had been feeling since he opened the door to the woman. He knew what he was looking at. Though as sheriff in his small town in Wyoming he hadn't seen many bullet holes in vehicles.

"Then there's this one." The old man pointed to the hood just below the windshield. Instead of scoring the metal, this bore a hole in it.

"No rusting," JT commented, examining the marking.

The mechanic shook his head. "It looks like it's recent."

JT raised the hood. Leaning over the engine block, he found the corresponding hole. After a minute of study, he stood back. "Looks like the bullet's still there. Just leave it, and I'll be back later to get it."

"I won't touch it."

"Thanks. And Lou, don't mention this to anyone."

"Sure thing. You think that little lady was in the car when someone shot at it?"

That 'little lady' was taller than Lou, but that didn't lighten JT's thoughts. "I don't know, but I don't like the possibilities. See you in the morning."

He walked out spying the woman that sparked so many questions. She stood looking off in the distance. A cloak of despair hung heavy around her shoulders. He stopped behind her, again fighting the urge to wrap his arms around her and haul her back against him. The temptation to comfort her was getting stronger. Before he had to make a decision, she turned.

"Is anything wrong?"

He debated a moment about telling her about the bullet scores, then decided against it until he did a little more investigating. "No, I just thought maybe we'd take time to go give you a driving test."

"Driving test? How? I don't have any identification."

"It would just be a temporary for thirty days. Hopefully, it won't be that long to find out who you are, but this will give you some freedom until we do. Though it will only be for driving around here locally." He turned her in the direction of the sheriff's office. He wasn't sure where the idea had come from, or why he had said it, but with the spark of life that picked back up in her, he was glad he had.

"What do I have to do?"

"Pass the written test, eye exam and I'll give you a driving test. What's wrong?" He noticed the light dim in her eyes.

"What if I can't remember the answers or how to drive?"

"Then you don't get to drive, but let's wait and see before we worry about that."

Jana's missing memory didn't prove to be a problem. She aced the written test and though she was nervous sitting so close to JT, she made it through the driving test with no problem. So, with her temporary driver license in her pocket, they headed back to the newspaper office.

They only waited a few minutes for Ted to finish up. He asked Jana questions the whole time, conducting what Jana guessed was a subtle interview. Jana figured it must be the mark of a newspaperman. The only thing though, she didn't have the answers and the more she tried, the more her head hurt. She was relieved when JT called a stop to the interview.

Back at his office, with a copy of her picture, it didn't take him long to fax out the picture and prints, then they headed back to the ranch. JT was surprised how late they were. Tyler was home from school and had part of the chores already done. With Jana and JT's help, they finished in a half an hour, just in time to eat.

JT sat back at the dinner table and listened to Maggie quiz Jana about her trip to town. When Jana didn't mention buying anything, Maggie interrupted her. "You didn't go shopping?"

"No."

Maggie turned on him. "Jackson Thomas Termaine, where is your head? Do you expect this girl to go around in nothing but a pair of your old jeans, Tyler's sweater and a couple of old T-shirts?"

JT had to admit he hadn't given much thought to her clothes. He wasn't going to admit that it had taken him a lot of effort not to think of it. "You're right, I'm sorry. I have to work in the morning, and I'm on patrol in the afternoon, but I should be able to get her to town for an hour or so in the late afternoon."

"That will have to do. I have a ladies group meeting here in the morning so I can't take her," Maggie said.

"Tomorrow's Saturday, I can take her," Tyler volunteered. "I can show her all around town."

"That will work," Maggie spoke before JT could. "You'd have to drive the farm truck. I'll need the other vehicle to pick up a couple of the ladies. JT, of course, will have his, unless, JT, you could take the farm truck."

"No," Jana cut in. "I can take it."

"You sure?" JT couldn't help his surprise. His ex-wife wouldn't be caught dead riding in something like the farm truck, much less driving it.

She nodded without hesitation.

"Will three hundred be enough?" he asked.

"Three hundred?" She looked back.

"Yeah, can you get what you need for that?" His ex-wife could easily blow that on one outfit, but there weren't shops with that kind of prices around town.

Jana shook her head.

"Four?" JT said, feeling a wave of disgust at women and their clothes.

"I don't need that much and I don't know when I can repay you."

"You'll repay me when you can. Now, how much do you think you'll need?" JT didn't know why he was feeling such irritation now that she was refusing his money.

In his experience, women always wanted gifts and money from men. He had seen enough of it when he was in D.C., and it usually led to trouble. For some reason though, he wanted Jana to depend on him even if it was just to get some clothes.

"Could … could I borrow a hundred?"

The effort in which it took her to ask told him she wasn't used to asking for things. Jana was self-sufficient. "You sure that's enough?"

"Yes, thank you. I just need a few things," she assured.

"All right." He left the room going into his den and came back with the money and handed her five crisp twenties. "If that isn't enough, stop by the sheriff's office, or you can have the shopkeepers charge it and I'll stop by and pay it later."

She nodded, but said, "I'm sure this will be fine. If

you'll excuse me, I think I'll help with the dishes then go to bed early."

Maggie turned from where she was running water in the sink. "Are you feeling all right, dear?"

"Yes. I just have a little headache."

"Why don't you head to bed, I'll do these."

"No, I can help." Jana gathered a load and carried them to the sink.

JT watched the women work together as he finished his dessert. The two of them found a rhythm in each other's movements.

Tyler brought his homework to the table. Several times he caught his son watching Jana. JT felt another twinge of unease, worried that his son might be turning to Jana for the feminine attention he missed from his own mother.

When, on a trip to the table for dishes, Jana glanced down and pointed out an error in his math then ruffled Tyler's hair, JT decided he'd better say something, yet the glow on Tyler's face stilled the thought.

 CRBO

Jana was running down the hallway. The shadows were closing in, reaching for her, catching her with their dark, misty fingers. She struggled, fighting to break free. Ahead of her the polished door stood out, drawing her in, but the harder she ran the farther away it seemed. She'd almost reached it when it swung open...

Jana shot up in bed, gasping for air. Her body shook violently. The terror faded as she could make out the room around the bed. The antique furniture and handmade quilt brought warmth that started to melt the ice that filled her body.

Too uneasy to try to go back to sleep, Jana slid from the bed and reached for the thick, navy blue robe that lay across the foot of the bed. She pressed her face into the velour, taking in the scent of the man she couldn't stop thinking about. Comfort spread around her as she wrapped herself in it. Looking back at the bed, she wondered if she could manage to go back to sleep but knew it would be impossible.

Jana sat down on the edge of the bed and pulled on a pair of socks before heading for the kitchen. In the hall, she froze, when she caught sight of light coming from JT's den. The scene was so much like her dream, Jana almost turned and fled, but before she could make her feet move, JT stepped into the hallway.

"Jana," he immediately picked her out in the darkness. "Is something wrong?"

"I was getting a drink." She kept her voice to a whisper, making her way to him.

"I'll join you." He fell in step with her, taking her arm to guide her through the darkness of the family room, when she slowed her pace. "Would you like a hot chocolate?"

Jana was about to decline then, being honest, answered. "Yes, please." She hoped the soothing warmth would help her sleep. She was surprised to find it was only a quarter to twelve. "You're up late," she commented.

"Working on books for the ranch." He walked around the kitchen, talking to her while he filled the kettle. Jana got the cups, spoons and mix. They worked in perfect harmony. Intimacy hung thick in the air, but neither commented on it.

Jana hunted for a subject to break the tension. "It must be hard running the ranch and being the sheriff. They both seem to be full-time jobs."

"Yeah, they take up a lot of time, but I couldn't give up either."

"They're both part of you."

"Yeah, it took me years to realize I couldn't live without the ranch, the feel, the freedom, and the outdoors. It's all part of me, though I always wanted to be in law. I even toyed with being a lawyer."

"You did? I don't think I could see you as one."

"It took me a while to realize that I couldn't either." He smiled at her wide-eyed look.

"How'd you end up as sheriff?"

"The long way."

When he fell silent, she didn't pry, figuring he didn't want to talk about it. She was surprised when he started.

"I'd just finished my second year of law school. I pushed my way through college as I did high school. Tested out of a few classes, then I took on an average of twenty to twenty-two credits. Now that I look at it, it was pretty crazy. I hardly had time for anything else. I was getting burned out, and realized being a lawyer wasn't for me. That's when I was scouted out by the FBI.

"I came back here before I went for training. And that's when I met Tyler's mother. She'd just turned nineteen and was beautiful. Now I realize it was lust at first sight." He dipped his head before he look back at her

"She was too young. She oohed and aahed over me. The next thing, I knew, I was married and heading off to training. I ended up top of the class in everything and landed a peach of an assignment. Six months into it, my supervisor was transferred to D.C. and took me with him. Marcy, my wife, loved it. She got to meet a lot of high-profile people." He grimaced at the memory.

"She wasn't really happy when she found out she was pregnant. I didn't understand that, but at least, she didn't try to end it. I knew another guy whose wife did that. She didn't even tell him until after."

"You're kidding," Jana gasped.

JT shook his head. "Anyway, even though Marcy hated what being pregnant did to her body, it was kind of 'vogue'," he made a gesture with his fingers as if putting the word in quotes, "to be pregnant at the time. And then when Ty came, he was so cute. He was a good baby, easy to show off, and it was still the popular thing. Her focus was to get back into shape and looking perfect."

He shifted in his chair. "Our marriage was pretty much just surviving by then. I was working all the time. She was going to luncheons, shopping. She volunteered on all the right committees, which let her meet very interesting people. Then Tyler started to get older, not making just the cute baby noises but louder and messier, getting into things. She was leaving him home with the babysitter more and more, days and nights. I had to spend a lot of time at work. I gave what I could to Ty, but I knew he wasn't getting enough attention.

"When I tried to talk to Marcy about it, she informed me that was not the life she wanted. She liked what she had in D.C. and wasn't going to give it up. So I tried to do more. It would be days between when I would see her. I was starting to miss the ranch, open space, and horses. That's when I started thinking of coming back, and then my dad told me about the sheriff's job opening up. I thought it would be perfect, and maybe if she got away from the influences there, that maybe we could make our marriage work."

His expression affirmed the negative before his words. "When I approached Marcy about it, she said, I could go if I wanted to. She had no desire to be a wife of a small town sheriff. She'd gotten out of that hick town USA and was never going back. That's when I knew for sure what I had come to suspect – that it was never going to work. She gave me the divorce and full custody of Tyler. I was uncontested as sheriff."

"Ever miss Washington?"

"Not at all." He looked up.

"I don't think I could live there either." She stopped. "I've been there." She gasped. "I had an image of the space capsule and the Smithsonian, the dinosaur exhibit, and Lincoln Memorial. I ... It's gone now."

"That's okay. What did you see?"

"It was a whole bunch of images, kind of like animated

photos. I saw my father, he was pointing out something to my brother. I have an older brother. I don't know their names but I know it was my brother. This is so frustrating." She reached up and rubbed her temples.

"It's coming though."

"Yeah, but is my family worried? Are they missing me, wondering where I am?" Jana swallowed, her voice broke. "I don't know which is worse. The thought of them being worried or that no one cares."

"Someone cares," JT assured her.

After a second, Jana raised her head and managed a watery smile. "Thanks."

"Anytime." He pulled back at the smile of gratitude she gave him. "I'd better go finish up my books." He excused himself, taking his cup to the sink.

"I'll clean up." Jana stood. The feeling of comfort she'd experienced a second earlier shattered.

"Thanks." JT retreated to his den.

It only took Jana a couple of minutes to tidy the kitchen. Quietly, she made her way down the hall, careful not to disturb the man who disturbed her so. Jackson Thomas Termaine played havoc with her emotional equilibrium.

One moment she felt the connection with him like no other, a comfort, warmth that went all the way to her soul, then the next instant, there would be a cold stone blockade freezing her out. Other times he'd look at her, and she felt as if she would burst into flames.

The remnant of the nightmare was gone. Her thoughts were on JT when she went to sleep.

❦

JT looked at the same entry he had been looking at when Jana had quietly made her way past his door twenty minutes earlier. He shoved back the books knowing it was no use tonight. The accounting side was never his favorite part of the ranch. He had enough of it in the sheriff's office.

If it wasn't so important, he would never do it at home.

Now, due to the woman sleeping in his guest room, making sense of entries was near impossible. She invaded his house, his thoughts, and his life. He couldn't believe what he'd revealed in the kitchen. It was something he never discussed. JT wasn't sure what hurt most with Marcy, being used and discarded, or his bad judgment in the first place.

Why did he have to tell her his life story? He was tired, that had to be it. He pushed back from his desk. Twenty minutes later and sleep wasn't any more successful than doing books had been.

The image of Jana wrapped in his robe took possession of his mind. She looked so fragile. He wondered if she'd had a nightmare.

He didn't want to think of that. He didn't want to think of her. He didn't know why he couldn't get her out of his thoughts. She wasn't gorgeous. But with the belt cinched tight at her waist and a pair of his socks on her feet, she'd looked so adorable.

She was a mystery and he loved a mystery. That had to be the draw, he tried to convince himself, but it wouldn't work. No matter how he tried, her image was there. She had taken up residency in his head just as she did in his life.

Chapter Six

Jana didn't think the farm truck was as bad as they'd made it sound. Yeah, the blue truck was old and a little banged up, but it wasn't rusted out and it ran well. With the turn of the key, it fired to life without a single sputter or groan. Ty was her proud navigator as they headed for town, telling her all about the area, school, and his friends. The town had about three thousand four hundred residents, but the surrounding area filled out another thousand.

"Does your brace make it difficult to drive?" Ty asked out of the blue.

"A little, but I think it's a lot better than a cast. I'll be happy to have it off in a couple of days. I'm lucky it wasn't broken. What's bothering me most is the stitches, they itch." She wrinkled her nose and grinned. "I need to ask Dr. Phillips when I can get them out."

"When I had my stitches last summer, I think it was about a week."

"How'd you get stitches?"

"In the barn. I was climbing on something and slipped, and I fell on a piece of metal. I got six stitches in my leg."

"Ouch," Jana said.

"Yeah."

They'd reached the center of town when Ty pointed to a parking space.

Jana started to pull in when she realized there wasn't enough room in the space left between the car and red line for the fire hydrants. "We're not going to fit. We can't park here."

"We'll only hangover a couple feet."

"That's still against the law. I guess I'm not very good at breaking the rules."

"Dad wouldn't give you a ticket and his deputies know his truck. They wouldn't either."

"Maybe not, but it doesn't make it right. And we can't use him like that. What do you think everyone would think of your dad if he let us break the law, or if they thought he did?"

"Not much."

"Your dad's a man of honor. We need to be the first ones to give him our respect by not putting him in difficult positions. Besides, how would he feel?"

'I understand. You're going to move, aren't you?"

"Yeah," she said pulling out. Halfway down the block there was an open space.

"There." Ty pointed. "In front of Johnson's Drugstore."

"This is much better." She maneuvered into the parking place then pointed to the sign in the store window that read "Ice cream". "See it pays to follow the rules."

"Johnson's has the best ice cream." Tyler's face lit up

She grinned, "It must be meant to be."

Tyler waited for her on the sidewalk. "I didn't bring any money with me."

"That's okay. My treat, after all, you volunteered your time to take me around. I think I can spare some of what your Dad gave me. I doubt he would mind, and I'll have plenty for clothes, but I think we need ice cream first." Laying her arm over his shoulder, she directed the boy inside.

છ૪ૺ

JT stood on the sidewalk and stared after Ty and Jana as they drove down the street. He watched as they got out of the truck and disappeared into the drugstore. She was definitely an intriguing lady. JT was unsure what to think about the obvious ease of her relationship with his son, but he couldn't find fault in the lesson he'd just heard her give through the open window, when he'd approached the truck from behind.

'*Your dad's a man of honor.*' The words echoed in his mind. He felt an odd twinge inside at the thought that she respected him. He walked a little straighter as he made his way down the street to the drugstore.

JT had no trouble finding the two in the back by the ice cream counter. It wasn't quite noon yet, but several people had already gathered there. Jana stood to the side licking a cone while Tyler leaned against the counter still trying to decide.

"I thought that you were clothes shopping," JT whispered in her ear, coming up behind her.

Jana let out a little yelp and turned. A hand pressed to her chest as if to help her catch her breath, but she managed to hang on to her ice cream. "You scared me." A smile lit her face. "We are." She pointed to a light blue T-shirt with a caricature of a cowgirl sitting on her saddle in the middle of a dusty road while her horse trotted away. The caption above it read, '*I found myself in Wyoming*'. "Perfect, isn't it?"

JT couldn't hold in a short laugh.

"Hi, Dad." Ty looked over.

JT moved to his son and laid a hand on his shoulder. "Still trying to decide?"

Tyler looked up at his dad. "Nope, I decided on bubblegum and candy bar."

JT grimaced at the combination. He turned back to Jana. "No problem deciding?"

"Nope, I saw peanut-butter cup, and I knew it was my favorite."

"In a sugar cone," JT observed.

"Absolutely."

"Good?"

"Perfect."

"Two scoops of peanut-buttercup in a sugar cone, May," he said to the woman who just handed Tyler his cone. "How much do I owe you?" he asked, pulling out his wallet, "Their cones and the T-shirt, too."

"It's my treat." Jana cut in.

JT ignored her and handed over the money. "I got it." He turned back to her cutting her off further. "Save it for your clothes."

"But," she started to object again only to stop when he leaned toward her. Instead she said, "You don't like to lose, do you?"

"Nope." Accepting his change from the woman behind the counter, he dropped the coins in a jar on the counter, slid his wallet back into his pocket, and then took a taste of his ice cream. "Mmmm. Not bad." He took a larger bite. "Not bad at all."

Jana followed Tyler out of the store. JT trailed them, finding himself focused on the sway of her hips. She wore his shrunken jeans that had now been cut off to the right length for her and Tyler's sweater. Feeling his temperature rise, he jerked his eyes away, but they drifted right back. Forcing his attention up, it rested on her hair. The silky smoothness of it beckoned for him to run his fingers through it. She stepped into the sunlight, and her hair lit with gold fire.

The woman was still messing up his mind. He needed to get away from her and the effect she seemed to have over him. "Well, what have you two got planned?" he spoke, keeping it casual.

"I'm going to show her Burt's and Harding's and The Boutique," Ty told his father.

"First, we're just going to wander, so I can see what there is," Jana added.

"All right, I'll see you later." He headed the opposite

way back to the sheriff's office, leaving them to their task.

ൟൠ

It didn't take long for Jana to get familiar with the town. The people who greeted her were friendly when Tyler introduced her. It took them only a little over an hour to do a quick run through of all the stores in town that had any clothing, giving Jana the idea of where to find the things she needed and was interested in.

They were coming out of Burt's, where a royal blue blouse on the sale rack had caught her eye, when they heard someone calling Tyler's name. Three boys raced toward them, weaving excitedly through the people on the sidewalk.

"Ty, it's great that you're in town. We set up a baseball game," the boy that reached them first announced.

Immediately Tyler lit up, then his shoulders dropped and he shifted. "I can't play today. I'm taking Jana shopping. Jana, these are my friends Barry, Cade and Dale." He introduced them. "This is Jana. She had an accident and is staying with us. She needed some clothes so I'm taking her around and helping her."

To their credit, all the boys greeted her politely, but it was evident all the boys were disappointed Tyler couldn't join them. The downheartedness was even plainer on Tyler's face.

"You sure you can't come?" Dale asked. "We can share mitts if you don't have yours."

"It's in the truck, but I can't. I promised Jana I would help her."

She couldn't keep back a grin. "I don't see why you can't go play. You've already shown me where everything is, and we've visited all the stores. I've been introduced to everyone, and though I don't remember all their names, I think I should be just fine on my own. Besides, there's not much for you to do while I try on clothes, so you might as well go have some fun. I can come over and watch the rest of your game when I'm finished."

Ty eyes widen to the size of silver dollars. "You mean it?"

"Sure. Where do you play at?"

"The city park, it's just one block that way." He pointed to the east. "You can either drive over or there's a cut through between the buildings." He pointed to the opening.

"Great. When I'm done, I'll meet you there. In fact, if I have enough money left, I'll stop by the deli in the grocery store and get some stuff so we can have a picnic."

"All right, thanks, Jana." He threw his arms around her.

Jana was surprised he would feel comfortable doing it, especially in front of his friends, but it made her feel wonderful. He was a great boy. She felt herself choke up. "Hit a homer for me." She gave him a squeeze then released him.

"You got it."

"Hey, will you put this in the truck for me when you get your mitt." She handed him the two sacks with her shirts.

"Sure, bye." All the boys echoed the farewell as they ran off.

Jana watched them go. *Oh, to have a son like that.* At that minute she realized she'd come to love the boy. She didn't know how it had happened so fast, but it would break her heart to leave him when the time came. With a sigh, she forced a smile on her face and turned in the opposite direction.

Harding's was her next stop, where she was going to get some jeans. They had several ladies' styles. The choice was easy, a lighter toned one that fit comfortably but hugged her hips to perfection if she did say so herself. They made her legs look long and slender. She wondered what JT would think, if he even noticed.

She was being foolish. She slipped the jeans off and put back on the ones that she'd inherited from JT. Actually, if there wasn't so much extra at the waist, they didn't fit that bad. It was kind of like her fit in his life.

He didn't seem to have the same acceptance of her that his son did. Sometimes he would look at her and she would feel something there, and then other times it was like he could hardly tolerate her. Though, he was usually kind, at times he was brusque, not bothering to hide his desire to be as far away from her as he could.

She just didn't understand. She was drawn to him in a way that instinct said she had never been drawn to a man before. Jana let out another sigh over the older Termaine male, the one that confused her.

With the pants purchased, she headed for The Boutique, where most of the things she was interested in were at. Tyler had introduced her to Mrs. Mann when they'd stopped there earlier. The woman told her to call her by her first name, Ellen.

"You're back," Ellen greeted her as she entered.

"Yes, I wanted to try some things on," Jana greeted back.

"Where's your guide?"

"I lost him to baseball."

At Jana's answer, the women laughed. "They learn the idea about shopping with a woman early, don't they? Usually happens with most of my customers' husbands."

Jana joined in the laughter, moving around the shop. Where the other two stores had mostly jeans, with a few shirts, The Boutique had a nice selection for a small town, and her prices weren't bad either. Jana paused, wondering what she was comparing them to.

She stopped first at the sales rack. There were three pairs of slacks and two skirts and a dozen shirts that she decided to try on. Ellen waved her on to just take them all with her into the dressing room.

They talked as Jana tried them on and came out to check in front of the mirror. The choice of pants was easy. One didn't fit and the other wasn't great but the khaki pair looked pretty good.

The skirts were a harder choice, neither was bad. One was short and brown, and hugged her pretty good. Maybe too good, she decided. It showed more leg than she was used to showing. The other skirt was white, long to her mid-calf. It was trim over her waist and hips but tiered out to flow around her legs.

Jana turned back and forth, liking how it moved, and at sixty-six percent off, it was only thirteen dollars, two dollars more than the other skirt. After a minute of debate, she decided on the longer one. It would look good with a simple shell or T-shirt and could be worn with her tennis shoes.

Jana chose two French cut T-shirts, one navy and the other red. They were cheap and could be worn with the skirt or the pants. She also came up with another fitted blouse with a small pin stripe that was also on sale, and a mid-weight, scooped neck sweater that fit nicely. She gave her choices to Ellen.

That only left undergarments. She chose one of the less expensive bras, but the little bit of satin and lace fit well. She then went to look at the packaged socks.

○§○

JT entered The Boutique. It hadn't been hard for him to find Jana since she hadn't been in Harding, and The Boutique was the only other likely option. He didn't see Ty but Jana was hard to miss. He moved to Ellen at the counter. "How are you doing today?" he said softly, so as not to disturb the shopping.

"Pretty good."

His attention shifted to Jana. She skipped over the tiny lacey thong underwear that his wife always went for and picked up a package. He watched as Jana started for the

91

front of the store then stopped to look at a nightgown that caught her attention. It was a simple cut, short and virginal white. It had small cap sleeves and a deep V'd bodice. The satin material would hug her breasts and hips. It didn't take much for JT to imagine it in his mind. With a longing look, Jana let her finger slide over the soft material then she turned away.

"Oh." Her mouth made a perfect O as she saw him. "Hi."

"How's it going?"

"Just finishing up," she said with a blush as she laid the underwear on the counter for Ellen.

JT wasn't sure what shocked him more, her blush or his thought of seeing her with only those little bits of material covering her breasts. JT cleared his throat and his mind. "Where's Tyler?"

"I let him go play baseball. I was going to try on clothes and some of his friends came up and invited him. He was going to stay with me, but I didn't see any reason for him to. He'd already showed me around."

"You don't have to explain." JT cut her off, harder than he intended obviously, by the way she stepped back. He cursed himself under his breath. "Baseball is one of Tyler's most favorite things in life," he added in the soft tone, trying to take some of the sting out of it. "You made a friend for life."

Jana was quite certain the sheriff didn't like the thought and wasn't quite sure why. Deciding not to let it bother her right now, she turned to Ellen. "I think that's it." She hadn't noticed JT move closer until she felt his breath on her ear.

"You're not going to get the nightgown?" His hushed tone tickled her ear.

Her heart took off like a bronco out of the gate. She made the mistake of looking back into his eyes and felt her face become hot.

"No, I … I reached my limit." Jana couldn't still the quiver in her voice under JT's gaze.

"I could give you some more."

"No," Jana forced firmness in the answer and backed up against the counter, straightening her shoulders. "I'm fine with the T-shirt. The other would be a waste."

"It wouldn't be a waste." Even as close as he was, she barely heard him. Louder, he said, "Practical little thing, aren't you?"

Finding her composure, she stiffened. "Not so little." Her composure almost shattered when she heard his whisper again in her ear.

"No indeed."

Luckily, she was saved from having to form an answer by Ellen's return. She counted out eighty-seven dollars. The man ran hot and cold, she thought, waiting for the receipt. Before she could take the bags Ellen placed on the counter, JT reached for them.

"I've got them."

"That's unnecessary." Jana reached for them.

"Just finishing up for my son."

"I told him he could go."

"I know." JT directed her ahead of him, wondering what had gotten into him in the store. It was bad enough to have searched her out, but the conversation over the nightgown was way out of there for him. Even if Ellen couldn't hear, and wasn't normally a gossip, he could bet his actions were going to be all over town in an hour.

Outside he moved the conversation to a safer topic. "You got all this for under ninety dollars?"

"I lucked out. She had some nice things on her sale rack that fit. I got two more shirts than I planned on, but they were such a good price I was still able to stay in budget."

JT didn't want to be impressed, but after being married to Marcy, who wouldn't even consider looking at a sale rack and hardly knew the word budget toward the end, it was hard.

"What's the plan now?"

"I was going to stop at the deli and pick up a picnic lunch and go watch Tyler play."

"That sounds good. We'll drop these off at the truck first."

Jana looked openly shocked but didn't argue as he led the way.

At the deli, they picked up fried chicken, potato wedges and a macaroni fruit salad. At the cooler, JT got a root beer for him and Tyler. Jana added one for herself.

Jana was just thinking of how comfortable it was shopping with JT when a cold chill froze her body in mid-step.

"Jana." It took a second for JT's voice to penetrate her mind. "Jana, what is it?" His touch on her arm broke her from the daze.

"Sorry."

"What's wrong?" His hand was still on her arm, and she could feel the tension in him.

"Nothing." When he looked unconvinced, she added, "Just a funny feeling."

"A memory?"

"No, I don't think so. Anyway if it was, it was gone before I could lock onto it." She shrugged it off as they went to pay. Again JT pulled out his wallet, refusing to let her.

They stopped at the sheriff's office long enough for him to check in, tell them where he was going, and grab a couple of paper plates, plastic utensils, and a blanket that he kept there.

The game was in full swing when they got there. They settled on the grass just on the other side of the fence from third base.

Tyler waved from shortstop. They ate while they

watched, cheering for both sides since all the boys were friends. Tyler managed to hit her two home runs instead of just one. After the second, he said good-bye to his friends and ran over to join them.

"Nice hit, son," JT greeted as Ty flopped down beside them.

"Thanks." He reached for a chicken leg.

"Do you like baseball?" he asked Jana.

"I do," Jana answered. Certainty filled her as she caught flashes of her playing it and other sports. "I like all sports."

Before they could say more, JT's radio interrupted them. After taking the call, he said, "Sorry, got to go. See you at home." He hurried for the sheriff's office.

Jana and Tyler finished the picnic with Ty entertaining her with the action from the day's game and other sporting experiences.

"Ready to head for home?" Jana asked, gathering up their garbage.

"You're done shopping?"

"Yep." Jana climbed to her feet and walked over to the trash can. Just as she dropped the bag, a movement across the park caught her attention. For a brief moment, she met a man's gaze across the park before he turned away.

Sickness filled her body so rapidly she had to grab the can for balance. She seemed unable to bring air into her lungs. The next thing she knew, Tyler was by her side.

"Jana?"

"I'm okay."

"Should I get dad?"

"No." She shook her head and drew in a deep breath, letting it out slowly. "I'm fine, really." Jana forced a smile. "But I think I've had enough for one day."

"We can take a shortcut through Johnson's drugstore." He slid his arm around her waist as if to help her.

Her smile deepened, and she gave him a squeeze.

"There's a break in the fence in the left field that lets us into the back of their parking lot."

"You're the guide."

By the time they reached the store, Jana was feeling better, but she was happy to be heading back to the ranch. The only reason she paid any attention to the truck behind them was it was more beat up than JT's ranch truck. The next time she looked in the mirror, it had gained on her and was riding only about fifteen feet off her bumper. In the time it took glancing to the road ahead and back to the mirror, the truck had moved up within ten feet.

"I wish he'd hurry and pass," Jana said out loud, glancing back again. She couldn't see the driver because, even though they were driving away from the sun, the sunshade was down. As if the man had heard her comment about passing, he swung to the opposite lane and came up beside the truck bed.

"That guy is sure in a hurry for this road," Tyler agreed, shifting so he could see. "Jana, look out!" Ty yelled.

Before she had a chance to react, the truck jerked as the other truck smashed against the back end. The steering wheel wrenched in her hands, but luckily she had both hands locked on the wheel and was able to keep control. She'd just straightened out as the next hit came, harder this time. Metal scraped and groaned. The pickup jerked and slid.

Ty cried out.

A small scream escaped from Jana as she unconsciously held her breath fighting with the wheel to keep them on the road. She slowed and tried to move out of his way, but it was useless. The other driver pressed down on his accelerator, smashing into her tail-end pushing it toward the side of the road.

"What is he doing?" Jana yelled, as the back end bounced off the pavement. The wheel jerked in her hands.

She fought to hold on, but there was nothing she could do to stop the truck from sliding off the edge of the embankment. It spun sideways and then whipped backward in a sickening ride down the slope.

How the truck didn't roll, she didn't know. It bounced, jerked, and swayed, jostling its occupants around before it finally came to a bone-jarring rest. Jana sat frozen, looking out the window and getting a good view of the other truck speeding away back toward town.

"Ty." Her throat was tight, and she couldn't get out more.

"I'm okay." The young voice was shaky, but it was the sweetest sound she'd ever heard, and with it, what strength she had left melted. Dropping her head to her hands still locked on the steering wheel, she sucked in air. She heard the click of the seatbelt release.

"Are you all right?" He slid over and touched her arm.

"Yeah." Jana turned, wrapping her arms around Ty's lean shoulders, hauling him to her, giving him a hard hug. She leaned back and ran a hand over his cheek. "Are you sure you're okay?" Her eyes searched him, looking for any sign of damage.

"I'm okay, but your head's bleeding again up by your stitches."

Jana raised her hand and felt the moisture seeping out from under the bandage. "I think I hit my head on the window. But, at least we're alive. I was hoping to have the stitches out by Monday." She tried to sound upbeat, but her insides were still shaking.

"That was Mr. Jenkins' truck. He drinks," Tyler announced.

"And your dad lets him drive?" Jana couldn't keep back her disbelief.

"No. Actually, Mr. Jenkins usually goes to the sheriff's office and sleeps it off. Dad has a bunk in the back room for him," Tyler confided, and Jana thought that sounded more like what his father would do.

"Well, he didn't use it today. And, he didn't stop, so we'd better see what the damage is." Jana fought to be as calm as possible for Tyler, who she figured was handling their accident better than she was.

The backside of the truck had huge dents, and one piece of metal had been shoved in the tire, shredding it. Jana wondered if, since it had been on the uphill side, it had kept them from rolling. If it'd been on the other side, they would have flipped for sure. She shuddered at the thought.

"We're not going anywhere. Your dad's going to kill me." She groaned.

"It wasn't your fault," Tyler objected.

"Yeah, but look at his truck." She waved a hand at the rear end.

"Now, who's being unfair?" He looked back at her.

"Smart kid." A smile found its way to her lips, and she threw an arm around his shoulder, again hugging him to her. Jana looked down and tousled his hair. "So how far is it to the next house?"

He looked around. "Rainey's is about a mile from here, but there's a radio in the truck. Dad has it so they can get a hold of him, even if he's working out on the ranch. He taught me how to use it, but I'm only supposed to if it's an emergency."

"I think this can qualify."

Tyler climbed up in the seat and turned it on. It was already set to the right frequency. Jana watched as he lifted the mike and pushed the button. "Dad," he waited a second, and then repeated, "Dad."

There was some static then with a rush of relief JT's voice. "Tyler, what's wrong?"

"We had an accident."

Chapter Seven

When JT heard Tyler call him over the radio, his heart lurched. He knew it was trouble because Tyler had been instructed never to touch it unless it was an emergency. He made it across the office before Alice could answer.

Fear ripped through him at the word "accident". A fissure of relief crept in that Ty was able to make the call and sounded normal.

"Are you all right?" He added a prayer for it to be so.

"We're fine, but we're stuck."

JT sagged back against the desk with relief. "Where?"

"Just before Rainey's."

"I'm on my way." He headed out the door on a run.

It took him five minutes to make it to them. He was out the door almost before the sheriff's vehicle came to a complete stop. He had seen so many accidents over the years and visions of what could have happened had been racing through his mind along with the recrimination at letting Jana drive.

He reached Ty first. "Are you all right?" He grabbed him by the shoulders and hugged him to him before pushing him away to look him over.

"I'm fine, Dad."

JT looked over at Jana sitting on the pickup seat, her legs angled out the open door. Her complexion was pale. She looked shaken. "Are you all right?"

She went to nod then lifted a trembling hand to her forehead.

"Here, let me see that." He stepped to her, catching her

hand and pulling it away. He removed the bandage, revealing where blood oozed around one of the stitches, and there was swelling again.

"What did you do?" He bit out the words.

"Hit my head on the window." Her voice was shaken.

"I can see that. I meant the truck. How could you run off the road? You should have said something if you weren't up to driving."

"I … I." Tears and anger rose at once, but it was the anger that won out. "What do you mean? It wasn't my fault. I tried but –"

"My son was in the truck. You should have pulled over and called."

"I was trying to."

They both were talking at once.

"Dad," Tyler yelled and caught his father's arm. "Dad, it wasn't her fault. The other truck hit us."

A moment of silence filled the air. JT looked at his son. "What other truck?"

"Mr. Jenkins, but he left."

"Jenkins?"

Ty nodded. "He hit the back of the truck. Jana tried, but he pushed us off the road."

JT looked at the crumpled side of the truck then back to the woman. Her anger was gone and it looked like it took the rest of her strength with it. If possible, she was paler. Her shoulders slumped, and her eyes were bright with tears.

"I'm sorry," was all he could manage to get out.

A tear broke free and trickled down her cheek. He had his arms wrapped around her before the tear made it to her chin. Her body trembled violently as she pressed against him.

"I'm sorry," he repeated into her hair.

A sob burst out, and she pressed into him. He held her tight, waiting for her sobs to stop. He ran his hands over her back and met Ty's look, nodding that she was all right.

JT heard his deputy approach and stepped back, watching as she wiped her eyes.

"Sheriff?" Monty called getting out of the vehicle.

"They're all right." He turned away, walking to the back of the truck, inspecting the large dent and the shredded tire. JT had to swallow hard to keep from uttering several unpleasant oaths.

Ty came up to him.

"Are you sure it was Mr. Jenkin's truck?"

"I'm sure. I know the truck, Dad."

"What was he doing out this way?" He reached out to squeeze Ty's shoulder.

Jana had gotten off the seat to come to them. "I'm sorry about your truck." Her eyes were dry now, but she still seemed unsteady.

"Forget the truck. A few more dents won't hurt it. Besides, the insurance will take care of it. Ty gave me a description of the truck, but I need you to give me one too, then I'll have you tell me exactly what happened."

Jana nodded, taking a deep calming breath. "The pickup was older than yours. It had a big heavy metal grill on the front. Not a store bought, but the kind like from a machine shop or that someone who is into welding makes. The body was red, but it had some large gray primer patches. I couldn't see the man driving because the sunshade was down."

"Okay, that's a good description." Turning, he addressed his deputy, "Monty, I want Lloyd Jenkins brought in." JT turned back to Jana and his son. "There's no reason to stay out here. We can go home, and you can give me a full report there."

"What about your truck?"

"I'll call Lou at the garage. He'll have to tow it. I'll get your bags. You get in the cruiser."

At the ranch, Jana and Tyler each took turns in JT's den telling what happened. Doc arrived to check Jana's head. He had to redo a stitch. After reassuring that she would be fine, he threatened her about messing with his handiwork. He gave her two ibuprofen and told her to go lie down.

JT watched her head for her room. She still looked pale. Ty, on the other hand, jumped around like nothing had happened.

JT stopped at the garage to talk to Lou about the truck and spent a few minutes talking about Jana's car before heading to the office. Since his truck and family were involved, he left the recording he made of Jana and Ty on Monty's desk for him to write the report.

He was still at his desk went the deputy entered. "No sign of Lloyd. He wasn't at home and I can't find his truck in town. Gerald is still looking for him."

"Thanks, you want to type this up? I still can't figure out what was in Lloyd's mind. They we're both in agreement about the details, and it almost sounds like he ran them off the road on purpose."

JT fisted his hands by his legs. "It would probably be better if I wasn't around when you bring him in. They're lucky to be alive. It wasn't that he hit them once. He hit them multiple times, and then stayed with them until he pushed them off the road."

"You haven't had an argument with Lloyd have you? I mean, if he was drunk and thought it was you."

"No. I thought of that myself, but I just can't see it. Besides, Lloyd's not a mean drunk. Anyway, I'm heading home. I feel a strong need to be with my son." He also wanted to check on Jana, but he wouldn't admit that aloud.

The sun was beginning to drop in the sky when he turned down the lane to his house. The desire to comfort and protect raced through him, it slipped as he pulled the SUV to a stop.

The pair in the yard took him totally by surprise. The image of his boy needing his father, and the memories of the pale and shaken woman dissolved as his son laughed as Jana awkwardly caught the ball in the glove that barely fit on with the brace. She snatched the ball out of the mitt and threw it back with a surprising amount of speed and accuracy. Pride and pleasure blossomed color in her cheeks.

"Hi, Dad," Ty greeted.

"Didn't get enough baseball for one day." He teased his son while fighting the jealousy rising in his body.

"Are you kidding? Never. Jana's a pretty good catch, especially for wearing a brace."

As if to demonstrate, Tyler threw the ball, but in his haste, it went wide. Jana made a grab and missed, but JT was there catching the ball barehanded just before Jana ran into him. Automatically, his arm shot around her for balance, locking her to him as he took a couple staggering steps to regain his footing. Finally, he steadied and looked down at the flushed face of the woman plastered against his body.

Color blossomed on her cheeks. "Sorry." The word that escaped her lips was weak and breathless, adding to the desire roaring through his body. He wanted to take possession of those moist lips offered up to him just a scant few inches from his. He longed to run his hands up over her back, caress the curves of her, and wipe away the years of loneliness in her sweet body.

Abruptly he pushed her away, feeling singed by the energy that coursed between them, which he didn't want to acknowledge. She stumbled slightly, but he didn't reach to steady her. He watched the hurt and uncertainty cross her face before she tightened her control, pulling her guard around her leaving her face void of any expression. JT felt bereft, watching her close away emotionally from him, but that was what he wanted. Wasn't it?

Turning his attention from her, he tossed his son the ball. "Can I join in?"

"Sure." Ty lit up.

"Here, you'll need your mitt," Jana said working the leather glove off her hand.

"That's not necessary." He didn't take it as she held it out to him.

"I'm heading in anyway." Pressing the mitt into his hands, she turned to the house. JT hesitated a moment before sliding his hand into the leather warmed by her fingers.

⋐⋑

Jana heard the sound of the ball slapping into the leather mitt as she stepped into the house. She made it to her room before the first tears trickled from her eyes. She just couldn't understand the man. One minute he made her feel a longing like she knew she'd never experienced before, the next, his look iced her like the late spring frost did the first tender buds.

She tried to tell herself it didn't matter what Sheriff Jackson Thomas Termaine thought of her, but her heart said different. Jana wondered, if it was because she couldn't remember dealing with men, why it hurt so much. No matter how hard she tried to lay the blame on her missing past, it wouldn't work because she knew she had never had this feeling before. JT filled a place in her heart that had forever been empty. But, she refused to let the man rule over her.

Checking the hall to make sure it was clear, she ducked into the bathroom. The cold water doused the heat from her cheeks. Still, she gave herself several minutes to get control of her wild emotions before heading to the kitchen to help Maggie.

Dinner was a tense affair that night. It was a relief when, after dinner, JT challenged Ty in a game. Jana refused Maggie's coaxing to join them. Instead, she urged Maggie to play. It ended that they both did dishes so they could join the game. Jana didn't relish the thought of spending the evening in JT's company, but as they settled down in games, the evening passed fast and fun. It was late when they quit for bed. With a smile on her lips, Jana stood to receive a big hug from Tyler.

"Night, Jana."

"Goodnight," Jana said, turning back to JT. Quickly, she repeated the "goodnight" and turned to leave.

"Wait." JT cut off her retreat. "I'd like to speak with you a moment."

Jana didn't want to face him but refused to cower. "Yes?"

"Come into the kitchen." He strode away, leaving her to follow. For a second, she entertained the thought of fleeing to her room but quickly disregarded the idea, fearing the repercussion.

"Yes?" she said, entering the kitchen.

"I want to talk to you about Tyler," he began curtly.

Jana wasn't sure what to say. He didn't give her an opportunity. "I want you to stay away from him."

Jana knew he wasn't pleased with her, but she was totally taken back by the order. "What?"

"I said I want you to stay away from my son. His mother left him, abandoned him basically. While she was around, she gave him little thought and attention, absolutely no love. He hasn't had attention from a woman like you're giving him. I will not have him hurt by you."

"I have no intention of hurting Tyler. He's a wonderful boy. I would never do anything to harm him."

"With every look, every minute of time you spend with him, you're hurting him," JT bit out, fiery accusation shot from his eyes. "When you leave, and you will leave, you're going to rip him apart. He's a little boy who, for the first time in his life, is basking in a woman's attention. He's lapping it up like a starved little puppy. Your play, your dalliance is nothing to you, but to him, it's serious. I won't have you tearing him apart when you no longer have time for him."

"That won't happen." Jana tried to object.

"Won't it?" he challenged.

"No," she cried.

"The minute you find out who you are and where you're from, you'll be gone back to your life. You won't even remember being here. It will all become a dream."

"No." Tears raised in her eyes, as much at the thought of leaving, as to his words.

"Yes," he said sharply. "Yes." He lowered his voice. "So stay away from my son and stay away from me."

Pain ripped through Jana so forcefully she thought she would die on the spot. Her first steps backward were taken unconsciously, her mind trying feverishly to block out the pain. When that didn't work, she turned and fled.

Hot tears stung her cheeks. Breathing was agony. She fell onto the beautiful handmade quilt, letting it take her sobs, but it brought more pain. The quilt was made of love, and there was no love there for her.

Staggering to her feet, she grabbed her overnight case and shoved the items from the dresser into it. Opening the closet, she froze. The clothing that she hung there earlier that day mocked her. They were not hers any more than anything or anyone else in the house. Tears flowed harder.

Chapter Eight

The harshness of his words echoed in JT's head. And he wondered if the pain filled look on Jana's face would haunt him all his days. JT stiffened his resolve. Ty would be saved from pain, and maybe so would he, though at the moment, it didn't feel much like it. He was afraid it was too late for him. Jana seemed to have burned a space in his heart. He shook his head in denial.

Out in the hall, he heard the whisper of her retreating footsteps. By the time the sound died down, a heavy feeling settled in his heart. It was probably too late to save Tyler and positively too late to save himself from the awful pain and loneliness her leaving would bring. It hit him hard. He took a deep breath. Shoving his fingers in his hair, then bringing his hands down to cover his eyes, he finally admitted to himself that he was already in love with Jana.

JT had no idea how long he stared out the kitchen window looking for an answer that wasn't there. With a shake of his head, he decided he was better off without love.

He walked through the house turning off lights and locking the doors. The light coming from the cracked open door on the guest room caught his attention. He paused outside, knowing he should just go on, but he couldn't.

The sound of objects crashing together had his hand pressing the door open. He watched Jana set her overnight bag on the bed then turn to the closet. There she froze. After a moment, she closed the door, turning away.

His eyes left her long enough to go to the overnight bag. It only took an instant to realize what was going on. Fear swamped him. "What do you think you're doing?" He hadn't realized he spoke in such a rough voice, until she jerked toward him.

It took three strides to reach her. The face that lifted defiantly to meet him was tear-streaked. The incredible blue eyes were puffy and rimmed with red.

"Packing." The word was sharp and cut deep in him. "But I realize none of its mine. All the tags are still on so you can return them and get your money back. I'll … I'll send you money to cover the others when I can." The words seemed to be forced out of her.

"And where will you go?"

"Anywhere away from here, somewhere where I won't endanger sweet little boys."

She caught back a breath JT figured was part a sob. He felt himself dying inside.

"You don't have to go."

"Yes, I do. You said as much yourself that it's better that I'm not here. I don't belong here." Her voice cracked.

"No," he objected, stepping closer.

She shifted back. "Yes, you don't want me here," she cried out.

Rage slammed through JT like a sledge hammer at her anguished cry. Grabbing her shoulders, he hauled her to him. His mouth descended, catching hers in a fierce demand. There was no fight in her. Her body was molded limply to his as his hand ran over her back.

When he finally raised his head to take in much needed air, it was almost a minute before her eyes opened.

"Does that feel like I don't want you?" He pressed his lips to hers again, this time gentler, briefer, but just as hungry. "I may not want to want you, but I do."

Taking her mouth again with desperate firmness, he drank of her like a man trying to quench a thirst. After a moment he slowed, savoring the taste and feel of her.

Gradually, between kisses, he started to talk. "I swear, I've wanted you from the moment you fell frozen in my arms. I watched while you gave love to my son like his mother never did, and I wanted you more, which reinforced the urge not to want you. But it was no good. I can't get you out of my mind." He ran kisses along her jaw and neck. "Or out of my heart."

This time when their lips met, hers joined in eagerly. Sliding one arm over her hips behind her legs, he swung her into his arms never breaking the kiss. He made it to the bed and followed her down onto it. He was in ecstasy at the feel of her against him as he memorized every curve of her body. He gloried in how it fit so perfectly to him.

His fingers slid in the silky gold of her hair. He found it as heavenly as he'd dreamed. He released her lips to run kisses down her neck where he was greeted with the smell of raspberries that escalated the need to devour her. Running his tongue along her collar bone, she hoarsely cried out his name.

"Easy, sweetheart." He came back to her lips with a quick kiss. "Everything's all right."

"What's … happening … to me? My heart … can't breathe … pounding," she gasped out, clinging to him, but her words ripped him back into reality faster than a cold shower could've done.

He froze.

"JT?" There was question in his name.

"It's all right, Jana." The words were stiff, but it was the only way they'd come out.

"You're still mad at me." Her trembling changed from desire to pain, and she pushed at him.

"No," he snapped then brushed his lips across her forehead. "No." He softened the word. "Sorry, darling." He tried to pull back, but the question in her eyes wouldn't let him go far.

He raised a hand to brush back the hair from the side of her face. "It's just that we can't. I can't do this to you right now. You're too vulnerable." He looked deep into her eyes and almost gave in. "I would never forgive myself if I took advantage of you."

"But ..."

The word nearly sent him over the edge, and he pressed a finger to her kiss swollen lips to keep her from continuing, knowing his resolve couldn't last. "We need answers first. I need to know you're mine – that you can be mine."

JT didn't know how he managed it, but he released her and rolled away, off the bed. He took two steps back, shoving his fingers into his hair to keep from reaching for her. "I don't ... we don't know if you're married." He didn't want to think of the possibility. He wanted to grab her up, to hide her away from the world, to keep her for himself.

"No."

For a moment pain ripped him as he thought that she had read his thoughts and didn't want the same thing.

"No," she repeated, with the firmness of certainty filling her voice. "I'm not married. I haven't even ever ... I know I've never ... I'm certain ..." her voice trailed off as if she felt suddenly embarrassed.

JT found himself smiling. Some of the tension left his body. If her face hadn't already been flushed from his lovemaking, he knew it would have burned with a blush. But his heart soared as he understood what she was saying.

"Why not?" He knew it was an absurd question for the moment, but it just came out.

"It was never right before."

The answer came so easily that JT believed it was the truth. He prayed it was true and not wishful thinking, so that she could actually be his. At the thought of her being his alone, giving him what she had no other man, he tried to suppress a groan, but it slipped out. He paced to the window, putting more space between them in an effort to keep from returning to the bed and taking her in his arms like he wanted to do.

When he looked back, she was still in the middle of the bed as if waiting for him, the words flowed. "All the more reason to wait, but I'm warning you. The day we know for sure that there's no one else, I'm going to marry you and make you mine."

JT realized it came out sounding like a threat and was a totally reckless thing to say, especially with the possibility Jana wasn't free, but he couldn't help it. Even with the past sting of his divorce, he meant it. He was going to marry her as soon as he could. Jana made him want to take the chance he never thought that he would again. She made him feel loved. Looking down at her on the bed almost broke his resolve. He wanted her more than he wanted his next breath.

"I think we better not have any more kissing."

"But …"

His hand shot up, stopping her, and he groaned. "Please, don't say it. I'm trying." He crossed the space between himself and the bed, swooping down to capture her kiss swollen lips again. His arms were braced on either side of her, keeping his body back. He wanted to lower himself, to wrap them around her.

With super human strength, he pushed himself back, tearing his lips from hers. "No more. Go to sleep," he commanded and fled from the room.

The hall was not far enough away, and one look to his bedroom said that wasn't either. He went out through the kitchen into the cool night air. He threw his head back and took huge gulps.

After a minute, he opened his eyes, staring up at the myriad of stars. Energy and desire surged through his body. He felt alive again. He drew in a deep breath.

There was nothing he could do about the desire, but there were things he could do about the energy. He turned to the barn. Two hours later he figured he had worked himself close enough to exhaustion that he might get to sleep.

ഗ൏ഌ

Jana's body hummed with desire long after he was gone. JT loved her. Maybe he hadn't said the words outright, but his actions and looks screamed them. And he said he wanted to marry her, to make her his.

She couldn't believe JT had said he'd marry her, but then again, maybe it shouldn't surprise her. He was a home and family kind of man. One who believed in commitment and that fidelity was important. He was the type of man she'd been waiting for. Why did she have to find him when she was missing half of herself? What did she have to offer such a man when she couldn't even give him her last name?

A flood of fear washed over her. What if her memory never came back? She shoved the doubts away. What if they could never find out who she was? She knew JT would never marry her until they knew for sure she was free. It probably wouldn't even be legal for her to marry until then.

Well, she would worry about that when it showed signs of happening. For now, it just gave her more incentive to try to remember.

Stripping the clothes from her overheated body, she pulled on JT's T-shirt and hugged it to her. Sliding under the covers, she cuddled down to replay every kiss, every caress, and every word in her mind.

The nightmare returned just before sunrise. Stalked by terrifying shadows, Jana sat up in bed with a start. It was several minutes before her breathing returned to normal.

She huddled back under the covers until the sun rose. Even her thoughts of JT couldn't push back the fear that seeped through her body. She wished she could go to him, be held safe to his body, but she couldn't put him in that situation. It wouldn't be fair when he was trying to be honorable.

At first light, she left her bed. The hot shower washed some of the chill of fear from her body. Once dressed and in the kitchen, she decided to treat everyone to a big breakfast. First, she started with making a breakfast crumb cake. With it in the oven, she cooked the bacon she'd found in the fridge. By the time the bacon smells filled the air, she could hear the occupants of the house stirring.

Tyler was the first one in the kitchen just as she was sautéing peppers and onions for the eggs. Maggie came in behind him. The eggs were in the pan when JT appeared, obviously fresh from his shower.

"Good morning, everyone." He placed a kiss on his aunt's cheek then made his way close to Jana.

She felt a wave of uncertainty, afraid she'd see in his eyes that during the night he had changed his mind. Her quick glance was caught and held. Her hand froze over the pan. The look in his eyes was so hot it melted away any doubts and the remaining fear from the nightmare. Jana felt her cheeks heat and flush.

JT grinned back wickedly, obviously catching her reaction. "And what are you up to?" His words were low and husky, only for her ears.

"Making breakfast. What would you like?"

His eyes flickered over her then back to meet her eyes. There was little doubt what he wanted, and her body reacted in an embarrassing way.

"I mean," her voice squeaked. "How would you like your eggs?"

JT grinned at the effect he had on her. He looked over his shoulder at his son and aunt then stepped so his body shielded their views. "Like in my dreams last night, in bed with you," he whispered in her ear, placing his hand over hers on the frying pan handle just before it slipped from her fingers. With the pan now resting on the burner, he released her hand and stepped back.

"Anyway you want to cook them," he announced, snitching a piece of bacon and settling at the table, with his son and Maggie.

The table was all set, with a vase of yellow Johnny jump-ups in the center. "You were up early this morning." He motioned to the flowers.

Immediately, he wondered if she'd had trouble sleeping and wondered if he was the trouble. Or, he paused, did she have another nightmare? He frowned. She'd had one two nights ago.

"Are you sure I can't help?" Maggie's question drew his attention.

"No, this is my treat," Jana answered, coming over to the table to set down the plate of bacon. Next, she brought juice and a square cake that looked and smelled like it was topped with cinnamon and brown sugar.

JT's stomach growled in anticipation. The last things she carried over were hash browns, and fluffy yellow eggs sprinkled with onions, peppers and topped with melted cheese. "Oh, yeah." Standing quickly, he pulled out the chair for her.

"Thank you," she said as she slid in the chair beside him.

He savored each mouthful of eggs while Tyler dug in like he'd about starved to death. Maggie complimented the cook. JT added his compliments, but as far as he was concerned, the strong, bright, beautiful, spirited woman didn't need any other good qualities, but cooking like this was a definite added bonus.

"Sunday morning breakfast should be special," Jana commented.

"It should. We usually go to church. It starts at nine o'clock if you'd like to join us?" JT watched her for an answer.

"Yes, thank you, I would," she said without hesitation.

The rest of the meal passed with everyone chatting about a wide variety of subjects. Each person put their own dishes in the dishwasher then pitched in to clean up before they went to change.

 G380

Jana wondered what JT would think of her outfit. Even though her tennis shoes looked okay with the flowing white skirt, she wished she'd bought a pair of white sandals. She pulled her hair up with a jeweled hair clip she found in her bag. The action felt normal as she twisted her hair, she figured that she'd done it often.

She used a light touch of blush and eye-shadow. The lip gloss she found was a soft, muted, rosy pink. The perfume in her bag had a touch musky and spicy smell, and she liked it, so obviously, her tastes hadn't change with her loss of memory. After a couple sprays, she pulled her confidence around her and opened the door, nervous how JT would perceive the effect.

G380

Finishing breakfast, JT hurried out to feed and water the horse in the corral, then release the two horses he figured would foal at any time into a small paddock by the barn. That accomplished, he headed back in to change into his suit.

Standing in front of the mirror, he ran his fingers back through his hair. What would Jana think? He'd gotten used to wearing suits when he was in the FBI and thought he looked pretty good in them, but all she'd seen him in were jeans or his sheriff's khakis.

He tugged one last time on his tie to straighten it before heading to the door. He paused in the hall. Jana's door was open, the bed was neatly made and the room was empty. He heard Ty in the bathroom so continued his way down the hall, glancing in the family room. When she

115

wasn't there, he moved into the living room.

Jana stood, staring out the living room window. Her hands were clasped in front of her. She had pulled her hair up in some kind of bun, but there were little wisps which had escaped free to kiss her neck as he longed to do.

She looked calm, at peace, perfect in the room, in his house. Her outfit was also perfect for her, soft, light, and beautiful. It hugged her figure, accentuating it without flaunting. When his eyes reached her tennis shoes, he smiled. There was a touch of sassy spirit, too.

Quietly, he moved behind her. Unable to help himself, he slid his arms around her waist. He figured she must have sensed he was there because she didn't jump. Slowly she turned in his arms, her sky blue eyes going right to his. Her eyes were so wide and such a deep blue, he found himself drowning in them.

"So beautiful." He didn't even realize he'd said it out loud until she smiled.

The bow of her lips spread up to the twinkling in her eyes. JT dipped his head to take her sweet, glistening lips. She met him halfway, ready to give back what she received. The light scent of her circled around him, followed by her arms, more tentative on his back than his were on hers, but there was no doubt about the acceptance of his embrace.

He brushed his lips along her cheek to her neck. The shudder that ran through her fanned the fire within him. Somehow he managed to pull back. Her head dropped to his shoulder, her breathing as rapid as his own. They stood silent until JT detected movement down the hall.

"I shouldn't have done that." At his voice, she lifted her face up. He almost groaned at the sight of her lips slightly swollen and missing most of the lipstick from his kisses.

He raised his hand to cup her cheek and ran his thumb over the sweet bow of her mouth. She responded by pressing her face into his palm and kissing his thumb while her eyes drifted close. He wondered if she knew what an innocent offering she looked like. He brushed his lips lightly over her eyelids.

Out of the corner of his eye, he saw Tyler and Maggie look into the room and then share a look of satisfaction and conspiracy before moving back down the hall.

CR&O

Jana felt JT start to move back. She wished the intimacy didn't have to end but knew it was time. The look of longing he gave her said he felt the same, and she almost sank back into him as his thumb brushed her lips again.

"I messed up your lipstick."

She couldn't keep the smile in. Reaching up, this time it was her turn to run her thumb across his lips to wipe away the smear. She gasped when his lips caught the appendage, nipping it lightly, his smile becoming wicked.

"Oh." She stared up, unable to look away from the sensuality of the moment until, as if she was a diver who had been holding her breath too long, she gasped in several large breaths. "I'll go fix it. Maybe it wasn't such a good idea to wear it."

"You look beautiful."

She stepped back and boldly looked him up and down. "You look pretty good yourself." Her bravo was spoiled by a blush. Tipping his head back, he laughed, and Jana made her escape down the hall. It took a minute to steady her thundering heart.

When she returned a few minutes later with her lip gloss fixed, she once more had her breathing back under control. "Sorry to keep you waiting," she said to the family, sneaking a peek at JT, who caught the look and grinned back.

"Nonsense, dear, you look lovely. Doesn't she JT?"

"Quite lovely," his voice hummed, making her legs go weak.

CRITICAL

Church was a pleasant affair. Afterward, everyone in town seemed to gather on the lawn to socialize in the beautiful spring sunshine. It was hard to believe that not even a week earlier the ground had been covered with a foot of snow.

Jana drew a lot of curiosity. The knowledge of her existence had spread through town like a wild fire, and it looked like everyone wanted a chance to meet the woman who'd appeared mysteriously without any memory. She enjoyed meeting the town's people who seemed so welcoming and friendly, but soon the names and faces began to swim through Jana's mind, overwhelming her.

JT mingled, never far and always conscious of her. He didn't miss the touch of her fingers to her temple. He knew the motion came when she was getting a headache. The smile that radiated up to her eyes had dimmed, though it didn't leave her lips.

Excusing himself, JT was at her side in a couple strides. Cupping his hand under her elbow, she turned to him. A look of relief swept over her.

"Ready to go?" he asked already knowing the answer.

She nodded and turned back to the group. "Good-bye. It was nice to meet you," she bid farewell.

"See you," JT said, drawing her away.

They were almost at the parking when he felt her slump slightly against his side. He was tempted to move his hand from under her elbow and slide it around her waist, but there was already so much speculation about their relationship, he wasn't going to give the fire any more fuel.

"Do you want to wait by the car while I get Maggie and Tyler?"

"Yes, please." The relief was heavy in her voice.

"Everyone's getting a bit too much?" It wasn't really a question since he was pretty sure he knew the answer.

"They're all very nice, but, yes. And I'm afraid, I'll

never remember half the names."

"It's all right. They won't be offended. It's just you're the most exciting thing to happen around here in a long time. We're a pretty quiet community, and a beautiful stranger with amnesia is the thing fantasies are made of."

"You mean if she falls in love with the handsome sheriff?"

His look was meaningful. "Precisely."

"I think it would be impossible for her not to." Her words were soft and breathless.

Their eyes locked and held. JT wanted to dip his head and take those sweet lips, obliterating her make-up again, like she was obliterating his self-control. He didn't care if the whole town was watching. Instead, he released her arm and stepped back.

"Wait here in the shade and I'll be right back." He forced himself to turn away.

ଔ୫ଓ

Jana leaned back against the hood of the car. A moment of peace was just what she needed. Between all the people vying for her attention and the emotions that JT caused, her system was on overload. She took a deep soothing breath. Wilson Butte was a nice town, well-kept, with friendly people. She liked it a lot.

She let her gaze run up and down the block. A shiver knifed through her body before she even really saw him. He was barely visible behind some bushes across the street. She could make out dark hair and a plain blue shirt, but the shadows obscured everything else. She didn't need more to know he was watching her. Her body numbed with overwhelming fear.

Panic filled her. She edged away, off the car, backing up, afraid to turn her back to him. The touch on her shoulder ignited the silent scream. Strength drained totally from her body. She would have fallen if it weren't for the hands that caught her.

"Sorry," JT chuckled. "I didn't mean scare you."

The laughter died from his voice when she turned to him. "Jana, what's wrong?"

All she could manage was to shake her head. She crumpled into him, needing the security his strong arms brought.

"Ty open the door. Let's get her sitting down." JT directed her into the car while Ty held the door.

"Jana?" Ty said her name just like his father had.

She still couldn't get out an answer. She dropped into the seat.

Chapter Nine

If JT hadn't known better, he'd say he was dealing with someone in shock. "Jana." He crouched in the opening to the car, patting her hand. "Jana, look at me." He released the breath he'd been holding when she finally turned her head. "Jana." He saw a shudder pass through her the moment she recognized him.

"What happened?" He kept his voice gentle.

Jana just stared for a moment then shook her head. A feeling of foolishness washed over her. She was in the middle of a church parking lot. The sun was shining, birds singing, people mingling all around, and she was having a panic attack. Still, she couldn't help but glance across the street, but saw no one now. Her body trembled as she managed to take a breath.

"Jana, what happened?" JT brushed her cheek.

"Nothing." She forced the word out.

"Don't tell me that," JT snapped, pulling his hand back. "Be honest with me."

She jerked, shocked at the hurt in the words, but he was right. If they were to have any relationship, she would have to be honest. She couldn't keep things from him even if it was just foolishness. "It really is … She stumbled over the words. "There was a man – watching me."

People had been watching her all day, JT thought. But there was no doubt this was different. Whoever it was disturbed her. "Did you recognize him?"

She shook her head. "No, I couldn't even see him very

well. He just frightened me."

JT once more picked up her hand. He rubbed his thumb over her knuckles. "Where is he?"

"He's gone now. He was over there across the street, behind those bushes."

"I'm going to have a look. Ty, will you stay with her? Aunt Maggie's going to ride home with Doc."

JT didn't see anything as he crossed the street, though, what he did see when he came around the bushes, made his heart pound. The grass was trampled down like someone had been standing there for a long time. There was no indication of who it might be, and a sweep around the house lead to no signs of anyone. He returned to the spot where the man was standing to check again for any clue of the person, there wasn't any.

He stood back up, looking across the road. He could see all the people gathered on the church lawn and Tyler talking to Jana, who was still seated in the car. She was out of his sight now, but earlier she would have been in plain view.

He couldn't help but wonder if whoever had been standing there had been watching her. If so, who was it? Why? And did they know who she was? Suddenly the need to find out the answers took on a whole new importance.

Jana was calmly talking to Ty when he returned to the car. "Did you find anyone?" Anxiety flashed back to taint her words.

"No, sorry."

"I'm sorry to freak out so. My mind is playing tricks on me. I guess the blanks are making me a little paranoid."

JT debated a second on saying anything but decided the same rule of honesty applied to him. "You're not paranoid. Someone had been there. There was just no sign of who it was."

JT decided his son was a master at diversion when Ty switched the subject to horses, announcing that he and Jana were planning on going for a ride when they got back to the ranch.

"That sounds great. We can turn it into a picnic," JT managed to get out. Unfortunately, he was having a hard time getting his thoughts away from why someone was watching Jana, if they really had been.

His mind was coming up with a multitude of possibilities, and his least favorite was the possibility Jana had an abusive husband after her. If that was true, if she was fleeing, then she wouldn't be free to marry him. It also meant that, when she got her memories back, she might not be willing to take a chance on marriage again.

When the three reached the ranch, they quickly changed clothes. JT went to saddle the horses while Jana and Tyler made a lunch. Roast beef sandwiches, apples, cookies, pop and water bottles went into saddle bags. JT was doing up the last cinch when they showed up with the food.

"Thanks." He took the saddle bag and fastened it behind his saddle. He watched with satisfaction as Jana stopped by the horse's nose letting the big bay with black mane and tail sniff her hand, then laughed as the horse used her as a rubbing pole, nearly knocking her over.

"This knot-head is Duke." JT reached up to scratch the blaze between the animal's eyes. "He's my horse. That's Nickers." He pointed to a black and white pinto. "He's Ty's. His grandfather gave him to him. This little lady," he directed her to another beautiful bay, "is Duchess. I hope you'll like her. She has the nicest trot and gallop a horse can have. She's gentle but still has a touch of spirit in her."

"Hi, Duchess." She repeated the action she used with Duke, but Duchess rubbed against her more lightly. "She's beautiful. She looks like my Dad's horse."

"Another glimpse?"

"Yes, I was younger than Ty's age, and we were going riding. It was a sunny spring morning, much like this one.

But, it's gone now. I think Duchess and I will get along perfectly."

The words repeated in his mind, but he was looking at the woman, not the horse. He couldn't help thinking how they got along perfectly, now he wasn't trying to push her away. "Need a hand up?"

"I think I can manage." She gave him a cheeky smile. Placing her foot into the stirrup, she gripped the saddle and swung up in a fluid motion, giving JT a delicious view of her backside, hugged by the pair of his old jeans. Yup, those jeans were looking better than they ever did on him. Life was looking a little better, too.

"Cocky," he muttered at the look she sent down at him.

Jana threw back her head and laughed. She made a glorious sight on the horse. She should always look like that, full of laughter, bathed in sunlight. No fear, no worries, just joy shining around her.

JT raised his hand to her calf, giving it a light squeeze. Her gaze came back to him, giving him a private look that was so full of love it took his breath away, and left him praying that no other man had ever received a look like that from her before.

"Ready, Jana?" Ty asked from on top of Nickers."

There was a change in her smile, though it still remained loving when she looked to his son. JT felt his heart soar. Two days before, that look had filled him with worry. Today it added to his feeling of rightness about her.

"You bet. Your Dad is just checking my stirrup." She looked down at JT's hand on her calf.

He ran his hand over it before he went around to the other leg. He watched her as he repeated the process. "Looks good, feels that way, too," he said, his voice dropping low, before turning to his horse.

A minute later they were following Tyler across the pasture. They rode silent for a while before JT maneuvered his horse up beside her.

"You seem to be doing quite well."

"I think it's been awhile, but I know I like riding." Her sentence broke off. "Oh, antelope."

"We get a lot of them, deer too, and you'll occasionally see elk. No buffalo, not in the wild anyway, but I have a friend that raises them if you'd care to see one."

"It's so lovely out here."

"It has its moments," JT said with pride. "Actually we're on the edge of what is considered more of the barren part of the state. It gets dry in the summer, cold and snow in winter, some winds. It isn't always easy here, but there's something special about the land."

"The people, too." It was said so soft, JT wasn't sure she'd actually said it. She was looking off in the distance.

They had been riding about forty-five minutes when they stopped for lunch. It hadn't seemed like they had gone very far, but when Jana stepped down, she felt a few twinges in her leg muscles.

"You all right?" JT came up behind her with the saddle bag and blanket swung over his shoulder.

"It's definitely been a long time since I've been on a horse."

"We'll have to fix that, won't we, Ty." JT winked to his son. "There's a nice picnic spot right over here by the creek." He took her hand. "Right now the water is high with the run-off, but even in mid-summer, it keeps a nice stream. There's a little pool that's good for fishing and great for a cool-off on a hot summer day."

Jana felt her face flush. JT laughed, and she figured he had said it for the image to come to her.

Bushes and willow grew sporadically along the bank. A couple of large cottonwood trees towered over the picnic area. "The trees here were planted by my great-grandfather," he explained as he shook out the blanket. "The original cabin was right over there by the stream. You can see what's left of the fireplace. The house burned down so he moved closer to town, not far from the wooded area behind my house."

Both Termaine men took turns regaling her with tales of their ancestors, but when they got to the one about an attack by a jack-a-lope, Jana had to quash them by telling them she was familiar with the great western tease, where they took a small pair of deer antlers and put it on a jack rabbit to sell to tourists.

JT looked at the sky and sighed. "It looks like we have a fast moving storm coming in. We're going to have to hurry if we're going to make it back before it hits. We don't want to be caught on a horse if it begins to lightning."

He looked directly at Jana. "If the lightning gets close, get off the horse and lie on the ground. It's a lot better to get wet than getting hit by lightning, trying to make it home. A person on horseback is about the tallest thing out here." While he was giving instructions, they all were gathering up the picnic. "I hope you're ready for a run or at least a gallop."

"I'll keep up," she assured him.

"Tyler, you lead. Jana, keep him in sight. I'll bring up the rear."

Tyler set them off at a gallop then moved to a run. Jana figured he was making sure she could keep up, but there was no way she was going to hold them back. The ground passed rapidly beneath the horse's hooves. Jana leaned forward over the horse's neck and hung on.

She could hear JT's horse's heavy breathing blending in with hers. The horses seemed to know what was coming and needed little encouragement to head for home. They'd just passed the halfway point when the first streaks of lightning split the sky in the distance. Jana felt Duchess flinch under her.

"We're not going to make it," JT yelled.

Jana barely heard it before the wind whipped the words

away, but they were followed by a shrill, air piercing whistle. Tyler pulled to a stop and leaped to the ground. Jana slowed and stopped as she reached the boy, following his lead. JT's feet hit the ground, and he took the horse's reigns.

"Over there on the ground," he instructed, tying the horses to a row of small bushes before grabbing the blanket from the back of his horse. He ran to them.

Jana and Ty were already stretched out on the ground, and Jana had her arms locked around the boy. JT flipped the blanket out over them then slid underneath it, wrapping his strong arms around them both, pulling them securely to his body.

The sky lit up with electricity, putting on an awesome show for the trio. If Jana was supposed to be frightened, she'd forgotten to be. JT was curved the whole length of her body, her head rested against his arm. Tyler was snuggled similarly against her shoulder with Jana's arms encircling him, one of his small arms laid over hers and JT's arm over his. They were a unit. This was what a family was.

"Wow, did you see that one," Tyler exclaimed, showing no fear. The words were followed by a crash of thunder.

"Something else," JT agreed.

Jana could feel his breath against her cheek. "Incredible." She gasped as another streak etched the sky. This time it was JT's lips she felt on her cheek.

"We usually don't get many lightning storms in spring, they're more in summer. You can lie in bed and watch them race across the sky." JT's voice picked up a husky rumble like the thunder that rolled through her insides.

She knew for sure he was saying he wanted to watch them with her. Lightning was not the only electricity charging the air.

The lightning continued nearly a half hour before the

first drops of rain hit. A minute later it changed to hail. JT pulled the blanket up over their heads, and they huddled together, his body curving protectively over them as the small ice balls pelted the ground.

Jana gasped. "The horses."

"They'll be okay. They've faced it all before out in the open," JT assured her with words and a hand stroking from shoulder to elbow.

It was only a few minutes until the rain returned, this time, in big soaking drops. JT lifted the blanket and peered out. The lightning had moved on, but it looked like the rain was going to continue.

"We better make a run for it. We're going to be soaked either way."

Jana hated to leave what she felt there, but JT was right, they needed to get out of the storm. Still, she knew the time they'd spent in the storm would be one of her most cherished moments, one she knew she would never forget. There, in that pasture, she got a glimpse of the family she had always wanted.

She stood, going over the thoughts in her mind as she watched JT attempt to wipe down the saddles, but it did little good. They were all soaked to the skin in a matter of minutes.

"Keep it to a slow gallop," he said to Tyler. "It's getting muddy."

Fifteen minutes later, they rode into the yard. JT was there to catch her when Jana slid from her horse.

"You better go in and take a hot shower. Ty and I will brush down the horses."

"I can help."

"I'm afraid you better not." His eyes, which he had kept focused on her face until then, dipped down then back up. "I'm afraid you'd be more of a distraction then help at the moment."

"Oh," Jana felt heat flood back in her as she became

conscious of the way the wet shirt hugged her body, delineating her breasts.

"Oh, yes."

Jana couldn't think of anything else to say, so she fled.

JT watched her go, not feeling quite so cold. *Boy, but she could blush.* He was finding great pleasure in making her do it.

After taking a shower, JT entered the kitchen to find Jana and Ty at the table eating cookies.

"Jana made cookies," Ty greeted him, shoving one in his mouth.

"You bake, too. This is getting better and better." He snitched a cookie popping it in his mouth. "Mmm. Peanut-butter chocolate chip, I like."

"Have a seat, and I'll get your hot chocolate."

"I can get it."

"No, this is my special treat."

"Special treat?" He lifted an eyebrow suggestively.

"Not that kind of a special treat." She pushed him away as he closed in on her.

JT turned to the table to find Ty watching them with a smile that made him feel like he was getting his son's approval. Sharing a grin with his son, he settled in the chair. A second later, Jana placed a cup of hot chocolate in front of him and a plate of cookies. She then stood back, her arms folded, and watched expectantly.

"I take it you want me to taste this." He began to be nervous.

She just nodded, a funny smile cresting her lips. She glanced over and winked at Tyler.

Cautiously, he brought it to his lips and tentatively put his lips on the rim. Jana laughed at his actions. He wasn't sure what to expect when he sipped. The smooth, creamy taste was almost a surprise. "Mmm." He took another sip.

"Jana makes real good hot chocolate," Ty said. He too had been watching him.

"Wonderful," JT answered with another sip.

"Thank you." She curtsied playfully. "It's a secret recipe."

"Secret? What do I have to do to learn it?"

"I'll think about it." Her voice was full of sauciness when she turned away. He was about to make a sneak attack when the door opened, and Maggie entered with Dr. Phillips following behind.

"Oh, an excellent idea for a rainy day," Maggie said, seeing the cups.

"If you both take a seat, I'll serve you right up." Jana motioned them to the table.

"You don't have to do that."

"I insist, my specialty."

"A secret ingredient," JT cut in. "I was just about to find out what it is."

"Really, how interesting," Dr. Phillips said, taking a cookie. "A cocoa connoisseur. Do you have a favorite?"

"Mint Truffle is my favorite, but I like most milk chocolate," she said placing a cup in front of him.

He took a taste. "This is wonderful."

"Very," Maggie agreed. "You make your own?"

"Actually, it's the mix you had in the pantry. The trick is to get it really hot then put in a scoop of vanilla ice cream. That's what makes it so creamy."

"That's your secret recipe? You put ice cream in the hot chocolate," JT challenged.

"That's it."

"I thought that it was a big secret?"

"So, maybe I'm lousy at keeping secrets."

JT's cell phone rang before he could respond. He connected, listened a minute, then put the phone down. "I need to go into the office. I'm not sure how long I'll be gone. Don't hold dinner for me."

He crossed to the door then stopped. Striding back across the kitchen, he wrapped an arm around Jana pulling her up to him. Her mouth was partially open in surprise when he took her lips in a quick hard kiss. "Bye, Ty." He grinned at his son, when he broke the kiss and released her. Feeling very pleased with himself, he strode out, not even slowing as he snatched up his hat.

He knew Jana wasn't the only surprised person left behind. But, it felt so good.

By the time Jana recovered enough from the quick kiss that had about knocked her socks off, she wasn't sure what to say, but Maggie said it all for her.

"About time."

Chapter Ten

"Where is he?" JT demanded as he strode into the sheriff's office.

"Still in the supply room, sleeping it off." Gerald jumped to his feet.

JT took a deep breath an effort to keep himself from storming into the back room and beating the man to death. "Let's get him sober. I want to talk to him."

"Monty and I already tried to talk to him when we first found him. He said he'd been at the bar since yesterday about noon and was there until they closed and kicked him out. Said he stumbled into the back and went to sleep."

"Monty figured he must have come in when he was doing rounds for him to miss him. Anyway, since Jenkins said he'd been in the bar all day, we figured it would be easy to check it out. Lamar, himself, was on bar duty all day. He confirmed Lloyd got there about noon and didn't leave until quitting. Just like always, sitting in the corner, slowly getting drunk, as if it could block away Angie's death.

"Lamar is sure he didn't leave at all?"

"He's sure. I pressed on him how important it was. The thing is," the deputy paused. "His truck is missing. When we had him awake, I had him tell me where he parked it so I could check it for damages since Tyler was so certain. He said it was in his regular spot out back in the alley behind the bar. It's not there. You think someone could have stolen it?"

JT didn't like the thought of it, but couldn't see any

other explanation.

"You came down pretty hard on the Connor boy the other day," the deputy speculated. "Think this was his retaliation?"

JT would have liked to believe it was, but instinct said no. Worse was his instinct said that it had something to do with Jana, not him.

"Let's go sober Lloyd up and see if he saw or talked to anyone yesterday when he got to town."

Three cups of coffee and forty-eight minutes later, they had a mostly sober Lloyd Jenkins filling out a report on a stolen truck. JT headed over to talk to Lamar at the bar personally. Unfortunately, none of his questions yielded any more information than his inquires of Jana did. Lamar hadn't seen or noticed anyone around Lloyd, and he was positive Lloyd had been there all afternoon.

JT was beginning to get frustrated at not being able to get any information on Jana. Someone should have noticed something, and someone should be missing Jana.

It didn't surprise him that her fingerprints didn't yield anything, but her picture and description should have come up with something. She was too warm and caring not to have friends that would miss her. She did have a shy streak in her, but not enough to counter her friendliness. Jana was the type that did things for people, and that was the type people missed when they were not around.

He missed her, and he'd only been away from her for a few hours. What would it be like if she really did leave? He couldn't bear the thought and not just for Tyler's sake, but his own. He paused on the street, staring up at the sky. Now that the storm had blown through, the air was as crystal clear as his thoughts.

He loved Jana. There was no doubt in his mind. Just as there was no doubt that marrying her was right.

He shook his head and pulled his collar up against the cold. He bet that would really start a buzz around town when everyone found out he'd asked a woman to marry him after only knowing her a few days. Everyone would probably wonder if their sheriff had lost his mind.

Well, maybe he had because he was crazy for Jana, and the craziest thing was he couldn't even say why. She wasn't drop dead gorgeous like Tyler's mother. Though she was pretty, in more of the girl next-door way, but when she smiled or he looked into her eyes, she was beautiful. But it was more, there was something about her, something that drew him. He longed to head home. Instead, he made his way back to the office to go over Lloyd's report.

It was late when JT finally pulled into the yard. Most of the house was dark except the light in the kitchen. A plate laid waiting in the fridge for him to warm up. He wasn't particularly hungry, but he popped it into the microwave anyway. The kitchen felt lonely at the moment, so he took his dinner with him into the den. Tonight was a good time to go over the ranch records, to see if he could find his error and get the thing to balance.

CR80

The hallway went on forever and hundreds of doors lined it. Frantically, Jana tried each door, hoping one was open. She prayed she would find refuge from the demon chasing her.

She could feel him getting closer. Her heart beat wildly. She wanted to scream, but fear tightened around her throat making it impossible for any sound to escape.

At the end of the hall, a door stood partially open. "Please help me." She threw herself against it –

Jana shot up in the bed. Sweat soaked her shivering body. Her lungs burned as they fought to take in air. Tears streamed down her face.

She stumbled from the bed. The instinct to run was still with her, but she was afraid to open the door. It took her a second to understand it was not the door from her dream, and she was safe in JT's house. She wrapped her arms around herself and fought to still the shudders. Looking back to the bed, she knew she couldn't return to it, afraid the dreams would return.

The chill in the air added to the shivering in her body. She reached for JT's robe and pulled it around her, pressing her face into the soft material, breathing in his scent. It soothed her.

She wanted him and wondered if he was home. Not that it mattered. Even if he was at home, he would be asleep and there was no way she could go climb in bed with him, though it was tempting, almost too tempting.

Jana decided to make a fire, sitting by a warm fire, sipping hot chocolate had a definite appeal. She looked at the door again with trepidation. Shaking off the residual fear, she pulled on a pair of socks, tightened JT's robe around her, and forced her hand to reach for the knob. Still, it took all her strength of will to turn the knob, but when the door opened, everything was just as it should be. She pushed her foolishness aside and stepped out.

Jana was most of the way down the hall when she realized light spilled out of JT's office. She stopped in the doorway, feasting on the man whose head was bent over the ledgers, the pencil in his hand skimmed down the paper. When his head jerked up, she jumped, but the smile that flooded his face melted the last of her fears.

Unaware that she'd even moved, she was halfway across the room when he stood to meet her. Opening his arms, she walked around the desk and into them. Jana pressed her cheek to his chest, letting his powerful arms enfold her.

They stood silent, taking pleasure in each other for some time before he raised his hand to her cheek, tilting her face up to his. "Nightmare?"

She nodded, and he pulled her back to him. His hand ran up and down her back, stroking away the tension from her body. It was a while before she felt like moving. Lifting her head, she looked up at him.

"You're up late." A smile now made it to her lips, and this time she touched his cheek.

"Couldn't sleep. You can sit with me while I go over my books." Instead of directing her to a chair, he pulled her down in his lap. Jana rested her head on his shoulder. His arm cradled her back. There was a comfort, as if they had been doing it forever.

JT enjoyed the way Jana rested against him so he waited until he finished going over the next two pages before he asked the question he knew would disturb her. "Do you want to tell me about the dream?" He was right, she tensed, but after a minute, when he tightened his arms, she relaxed.

"It's the same as always. I'm running down this long hallway, lined with doors, but they're all locked. Something's chasing me. I'm too terrified to yell for help, in case it will find me, then I see this big set of double doors at the end of the hall. I start to open them, though I'm terrified of what is in there. That's when I wake up."

The whole time she had been talking he had been massaging her back. Now, he raised his hand to wipe away her tears. She sighed and snuggled against him, laying still.

"You're better than a fire."

He had thought she'd fallen asleep. "Huh?"

"When I got up, I was thinking it would be nice to start a fire and have a cup of hot chocolate. But you're much better than a fire."

"And the hot chocolate?"

"I'll have to tell you later." The playfulness was back in her voice.

"Oh, you will." He lifted her up so he could catch her lips with his.

"Much better," she murmured, when he lifted his lips. She rose up to kiss him. It was Jana that pulled back next. "I'm disturbing your work."

"You can disturb me any time." He attacked her with another kiss.

This time she didn't let it last. "If I'm quiet, can I stay here with you?"

JT was surprised she had to ask. He was tempted to say she could stay forever, but the future was still too unknown. "Sure."

She shifted so she was leaning back against him, watching quietly as he went over the page then turned to the next. Not that his mind was on the ledger anymore with her cuddled delectably in his lap. He was about to turn the page, when she reached out and caught his hand.

"You have an error." She pointed to a spot on the paper. "Unless you wrote this check number wrong, it should be in the other column as a credit."

JT couldn't believe it. Now that she pointed it out to him, he could see it, the error that had been plaguing his books for three weeks. She had found it just by glancing down at his books for a few minutes. The next words out of her mouth were even more surprising.

"I know this. The columns, the figures, I understand it all, and I'm good at it." She bolted forward in his lap, running her finger down over the entries with an almost loving touch. Lifting up a check from his desk she flipped the page coming to where it was entered. "See, but if you note it like this …" She picked up a pencil and wrote something. "It will be easier to cross reference, especially if you use a computer."

"You know about setting up records on the computer?"

"Oh, yes. I admit I still like doing it by hand, though. It seems people make more errors on the computer, though it's easier to fix them. But, I really like the old way. JT, would you let me go through your books for you? I can do it, I know I can, and it would be a way to let me repay you for all you've done for me."

"You don't have to repay me for anything," he said

firmly, but unable to resist the longing look in her eyes, he continued, "But if you'd like to go over my books you can. I'll warn you – you may be setting yourself up for more than you bargained for. I have a folder of entries that I've been waiting to do until I found my error."

JT could see he wasn't doing anything to dissuade her. "Come here. I haven't rewarded you for finding my mistake."

She turned to fit perfectly along his body, offering herself as his reward. He wasn't sure which one of them groaned deeper in their throat, but he guessed it was him. Either way, the sound echoed what he was feeling.

Jana was incredibly responsive. It was as if she was made specifically for him. If he believed in destiny or in soul mates, he knew she would be his. The feelings she brought out in him were almost scary.

He thought he had loved Marcy, but the feelings Jana raised in him were much more intense than he'd ever felt before. He almost wished he could say it was only lust, but that wouldn't be right because he knew it wasn't true.

Placing her on her feet, he stood. "Come on, darlin', I'll see you to your room then I'd better go to mine." His voice held a tone of regret.

They walked down the hall arm in arm. He was tempted to lead her into his room. Instead, he gave her a swift kiss and pushed her through the doorway.

"Dream of me." He knew it sounded like a command, but he didn't dare wait around for her reaction. He turned down the hall to his big, lonely bed. His mind still held the image of her sleeping there.

Chapter Eleven

"All done?" Maggie greeted Jana as she walked into the kitchen just before noon.

"Yes. JT keeps his records very organized so it was easy. They're all set for when he has to do his taxes. I filled out his itemized form for him. I hope he won't mind, but it will save him quite a bit over what he originally had listed."

"You know, if you're willing, I know Lou at the garage in town needs someone to do his books. His sister-in-law, Ruth, used to do them for him. But this year, since her husband's gone, she went down to stay with her sister in Arizona and won't be back for another month. He won't let the accountant in town do them. An old feud over the way the accountant takes care of his car."

"You think he'd hire me?" Jana could hardly believe the possibility.

"You could ask, but Lou always was a sucker for a woman in need. That's how he started having Ruth do the records, and she sure showed him a woman was as good as a man on the books. He's from the old school, and boy, did it take some convincing." Maggie chuckled. "In Lou's defense, that was thirty years ago. He's much more enlightened nowadays. One of his daughters is a mechanical engineer with an auto company."

"You don't happen to need to go to town today, do you?"

"I think I just might." The woman smiled.

Two hours later, Jana stepped from the garage and

headed to meet Maggie at the grocery store. Excitement bubbled in her. She had a job. Lou was more than willing to let her do his books in exchange for fixing her car and maybe some extra pay because, as he had warned, his records were quite a mess. Jana didn't care. She knew she could handle it.

She paused, drew in a deep breath, and looked around the town. It was a charming, well-tended town, where people knew each other and stopped to visit up and down the sidewalks. The shiver of awareness was a warm one, as if she had just found her own place in this town. That it was all as it was supposed to be. She hoped it wasn't just wishful thinking.

"You look happy?" Maggie caught her attention coming across the parking lot toward her.

"I am, it's all arranged. I'm going to start working on his books tomorrow. Lou said my car should be fixed by this evening. So, if JT will give me a lift in with him on the way to work in the morning, I can drive home."

൪൪

His ranch hand, Seth, was in the yard that evening when JT pulled in. "How's it going?" He greeted the old man.

"Looking pretty good, I'd say Daisy's going to drop her foal anytime now. Your little filly's in the barn with her now."

"My little …" JT started to question then it dawned on him what the old cowboy was talking about. JT tipped his hat. "Thanks, I'll just go in and check on Daisy."

"Why don't you? Ty's over at the Steadman's place working on a report. I think I'm going to talk Miss Maggie out of a piece of that cake she was baking earlier today."

There was no missing the hint that there would be no one to disturb him.

"Thanks, again." JT headed to the barn's side door so he could enter without making any noise. Jana wasn't by any of the stalls, but the sound of her voice led him to the stack of straw he left in the back corner.

"Here kitty, kitty." Jana's bottom wiggled in the air as she bent over a bale of straw, trying to catch the barn cat, which darted away. "You beast, if you're holding out for tuna forget it, it's not happening."

Sneaking up behind her, he waited then pounced. "Gotcha."

The shriek burst out of her, followed by her elbow swinging back. If it weren't for his training and quick reflexes, the elbow would have caught him in the jaw. It was all he could do to catch her flying arms when she turned on him like a wild cat.

"Easy, Jana. Jana it's all right, it's me."

She froze. Becoming so still, he was almost afraid she wasn't breathing. In a blink of an eye, she turned, and threw herself into his arms, taking him to the ground in the progress.

It was a tackle that would have done any professional football coach proud. Jana didn't seem to be the least bit concerned they were lying in the dirt and straw, and he sure wasn't going to complain while she was holding him tight and kissing him senseless.

"I was going to apologize for scaring you, but I think maybe I'll have to scare you more often." He growled out when they finally had to come up for air. Jana leaned over his chest, her hands locked onto his shirt.

She released him to smack his shoulder. "You can forget the scare part. I think that I just lost a couple years off my life."

"I think I gained a couple with that kiss. At least, I'm feeling a little younger and a lot more reckless than I have in a long time." He caught her mouth again.

"Mmm, I always wondered what a roll in the hay was like."

"Dusty," he grinned up at her.

"You're right." She sprang up, side-stepping the hand that reached for her.

He followed her to his feet. "You're in a good mood today."

"Doc took out my stitches. I did your books and filled out the itemized form on your taxes. I saved you some money to from what you had on your worksheet. You can go over it later, then all you need to do is sign it."

"Cheeky. That was fast." He was impressed.

"It was easy. You actually keep very organized records, though you did have a couple minor errors." She grinned back.

"You're enjoying yourself." He laughed. "But thank you very much."

"You're welcome." She glanced away then back again. "I also got a job today," she said quickly, as if afraid how he would respond.

JT was stunned. "A job?" he managed to get out.

She nodded. "With Lou at the garage. I'm doing his books. Maggie suggested it, and I went to talk to him. I'm working off my car repairs."

"You know, you didn't need to worry about that."

"Yes, I do. I need to feel worthwhile. That I'm useful, not just free loading or a non-entity."

JT nodded in understanding. "Okay, if that makes you feel better, but just so you know, I'm glad you're here."

"You weren't a couple days ago," she pointed out.

"A couple days ago I was still fighting with myself. I don't think it was ever you."

"I just don't want that to change. That you don't want me here, I mean, I'm afraid …"

JT reached out, caught her hands and intertwined their fingers, pulling her back to him. "It's not going to change because you are in here." He placed their hands over his heart. "I love you, Jana. I know it's sudden. It's been a long time since I've felt anything like this, and what I felt before is just a shadow of what I feel now. I love you, and if I could, I'd marry you this minute and keep you here in my own little world."

"That's the world I want."

"That might change. You have a whole other world out there you don't remember." He tried to be reasonable, though it hurt.

"I know my loving you won't change." She leaned into him. "And I love being here on the ranch, in this town. With you, Tyler and Maggie, it feels like home."

JT held her, wishing that it would always be true. "Did Seth leave me any chores?" he asked after a time and felt her shake her head against his chest.

"They're all done." She stepped away, taking his hand to lead him to a stall. "He said you'd get a new foal sometime in the next day."

"If Seth thinks she's that close, then it will probably be here before morning. Daisy's an old pro at this. The old girl's been having them since I wasn't much older than Tyler."

He opened the gate and stepped inside to greet the mare. "She's as good a mare as you could want, and her babies have been real fine, haven't they, Daisy?" He rubbed her neck. "How are you doing, old girl?" He ran his hands over the mare, checking her before stepping out.

"Come here." He stretched out his hand taking Jana's. "I want to show you something. JT led her through the barn. Jana made no objection when he drew her into the back stall, which was used for extra storage. In the back corner, he motioned her to look over to the lone bale of straw that was sitting kitty-corner.

Four little balls of fur were nestled behind it. There were two little gray and cream tabbies, and two others that looked like crosses between a gray toned Siamese and tabbies that caught Jana's attention immediately.

"Oh. How old?"

"Just over a week. They were born the night of the storm." The same night she arrived, it didn't seem possible it was only a week ago. "I forgot to tell Ty about them. He's been so excited about you being here I don't think he even noticed." The mama cat jumped up to be petted. "I'll tell him after dinner."

"She won't move them will she?"

"No, this is her space. She laid claim to it two years ago. She doesn't let us forget it. She's the only cat here that isn't fixed. Don't ask me why I don't have her done, but she only seems to have one batch of kittens every year, so that's not bad."

"Can I hold them?" She was already picking up one of the Siamese crosses.

"Sure." He smiled, watching her cuddle the tiny crying kitten which settled down once she tucked it under her chin. "Aren't you so adorable?"

"Looks like you've made a new a friend."

"I love animals. I figured that out."

"I figured that out, too. You'll have to come down and play with them. I don't want them to be wild."

The stuffy nose and sneezing hit Jana just as she stepped from the barn.

"Allergies?" JT asked, concerned.

"Never had them before," she answered without thinking. Sniffling again, she accepted a clean handkerchief from him.

"Let's get you inside out of the dust. We've been rolling all over the ground back there." He reached over and pulled a piece of straw from her hair and smiled. She definitely looked like they had been having an old fashioned roll in the hay.

He sighed. Unfortunately, it was all too innocent. Well, not too innocent, he thought of the kisses. JT almost laughed went she sneezed again. "I think you'd better head for the shower. Are you sure you don't have allergies?"

"I don't think so, but then again, I'm a mystery to myself. But it hasn't bothered me out in the barn before."

Through the evening JT kept an eye on her, as the sneezes became more frequent. After dinner, they sat around playing games and were just finishing up when JT got a call about a domestic disturbance in the bar. He only paused long enough to kiss her on the forehead and utter a quick goodbye over his shoulder before he was out the door.

"Ty, why don't you go put the game away and get ready for bed." Maggie said to the boy as JT left. Maggie waited until Ty was out of the room before she spoke again. "JT always has his deputies call when that happens. All domestic disputes can be dangerous, but bar disputes can turn ugly real fast. He likes to be there just in case," Maggie explained. "Being sheriff is a full-time job around here. That doesn't always mean regular hours." There was a pointed quality in her words that Jana didn't miss.

"Maggie," she looked over at the woman. "Are you trying to say something?"

"I am. I'm pulling for you. There's something about you I plain like, and there's something about you that disturbs JT – in a good way. That man needed some disturbing. He's been alone too long. He's not that kind of man. He needs a family. He needs a woman to love, and he needs to be loved by a woman. He never had that in his first marriage. The girl was too focused on herself to give anything to her husband and son. Oh, she could put on a good act, but that was all it ever was, an act. You're not like that. You're one of those people who, 'wear their heart on their sleeve'."

"It's that obvious?"

"That you love JT, yes. That's partly what got his back up and had him fighting you there for a couple days. I'd say you threw him for a loop. And the fact you obviously adored Tyler made it worse. What really got him though, was that you dug up long buried feelings, ones he didn't want to face. Boy, that man can be stubborn. I was afraid that he might chase you away before he realized what he had.

"I got kind of side tracked, but what I'm saying is, his life as sheriff here isn't always convenient or easy, but he's a good man. It'll take a lot of work, but life with him will be worth it. Now that he's figured it out, he'll love you like no man could."

From the moment Maggie started talking Jana had been overwhelmed. Now, all she could do was look at the older woman. "I do love him."

"I know." Maggie smiled.

"But Maggie, what do I do? JT's worried about what will happen when my memory comes back. That I'll remember there's someone else. I know there isn't anyone, but what if he's right about it changing the person I am now?"

"I don't think so. I'm not any kind of specialist. But I'm a pretty fair judge of character, and I think who I'm – that we're seeing, is the base person of your soul and shows a good person."

"I'm not so sure about that." Jana couldn't keep back the tears any longer. "I keep having these dreams. I'm frightened. I'm frightened they may be real."

"Have you told JT?"

"He knows about the nightmares, but I haven't said outright that I'm afraid they're real. This is the first time I've even admitted it to myself. When I was still kind of out of it the first day, I heard Doc say something about hysterical or traumatic amnesia. I don't think it was the accident that brought it on. I think something happened before. I think JT thinks that too. Maggie, what if I'm not a nice person? I don't want to bring trouble here."

"Now, hush on that. I already told you I thought you were a good person. And if there's trouble, there's no one better than JT to handle it. He's no simple country sheriff."

"I know that. I just don't want to see him hurt. I couldn't handle that." Tears streamed down her face.

The older woman came forward to give her a motherly hug. "Now, none of that. All I wanted to say was, I approve of you and JT. It pleases me. We sure did get off on a deep conversation. But you remember, don't go borrowing trouble. Everything's going to work out."

Maggie smiled, then her look changed to one of concern, and she laid her hand on Jana's brow. "You look a little flushed and seem to have picked up a runny nose that has nothing to do with those tears. Why don't you head to bed early? There's no telling when JT will return."

The thought of bed actually brought relief. Jana had to admit she was tired and had so much running through her mind. Down the hall, she stopped to say goodnight to Tyler before continuing to her room to change.

She stretched out and she thought about what Maggie had said. She understood why JT had almost run her off. Her smile deepened at the thought of JT loving her and Maggie's acceptance. The smile faded, though, when thoughts about her dreams surfaced. She burrowed deep into the covers to keep the shivers of fear at bay.

When the nightmare came jarring Jana awake, she remained huddled in her bed. She knew JT was home because the lights were off in the hall. She thought of seeking him out, but knew he needed his sleep.

Besides, he might question her about the dream, and she really didn't want to think about it, which she immediately did. It had been the worse one yet. The hall and doors hadn't been the only things. There'd been an explosion and a man turning to her, he'd been covered in blood and mouthed something to her.

Panic filled her along with the fear. Echoes of pain haunted her body. Jana rubbed her hand, then stopped, tracing the faint scar there. She studied it. It wasn't an old scar, though it was well healed. Still, not light like the others.

She reached back over her shoulder to where Doc had removed the stitches. How did she get a cut there? Her hand dropped to the back of her leg, and the healing section there. It didn't make any sense. She had seen the car. There were no broken windows, nothing to cause the cuts. She ran her fingers back through her hair, not sure if she was longing for the answers or not.

She wanted it all to go away. She wanted to stay here with JT, Tyler and Maggie. This was her home. These were the people she loved. The man she loved.

This was where she belonged, she knew it. She clung to those thoughts like a lifeline in the dark abyss.

Chapter Twelve

Her throat was scratchy when she woke up the next morning. She barely made it to the kitchen before JT entered.

"Hard night?" she choked out.

"Not any worse than yours, it sounds."

"I think those sniffles are turning into a cold. Can you believe it? I survive a blizzard, and then I catch a cold in a rainstorm."

"Are you feeling well enough to go to work? Maybe I should call Lou and tell him you won't be in today."

"No, I'll be fine."

"You sure?" He leaned over to kiss her forehead.

"Yes."

"Well, you don't seem to have a fever."

"I like your way of checking for a fever." She smiled, leaning into him to receive the hug as his arms slid around her.

"You can remember that for future use on me." JT ran his hands over her back and pressed another kiss on the side of her head.

"Planning on getting lots of temperatures?" she asked and sighed against his chest, enjoying the attention. It made the morning feel wonderful, even if she didn't feel very good.

"No, but you can always check to be certain." To her regret, his hands stopped their motion, and he leaned back to study her face. He must have been satisfied that she really was all right because he released her with a sigh of his own. "Okay, let's get some breakfast so we can get you to work."

○⑤◊

When Jana entered Lou's Garage, the old mechanic sheepishly pulled two overflowing shoe boxes from under the counter. "Those are from the last six months." He shifted like a child caught with his hand in the cookie jar, then scooted out of the office.

Jana smiled behind the man, then with a sigh, settled down to work. By noon she started to cough. Progress in going through the records was slow. She figured it would take a couple more days just to get them straightened out, but at least, she had the papers all sorted.

She got up and stepped out the door, letting the fresh spring air revive her before going back in to start recording the entries. Time passed without her noticing. When four o'clock came, her eyes were watering and her coughing was more persistent.

"You should head home and rest, girl," the craggy voice said from the doorway.

"Oh." She looked up, startled. Feeling her muscles protest, she glanced at the clock. "I didn't realize. I'm afraid you're right about going home. I did get you caught up through the New Year, so tomorrow I'll do your taxes. Then I will start to work on this year."

"That's fine. You've done a good job, young lady. I sure appreciate it."

"I appreciate you letting me work off my car repairs. I wasn't sure how I was going to cover it."

"That was no worry. Sheriff told me he would cover it that first day, if need be. So I wasn't worried."

Jana wasn't sure what to say to that, but the old man just continued.

"It's sure nice seeing the sheriff take such an interest in you. I thought that woman he got caught with the first time around spoiled him for women, which was a real shame. He was always such a good kid. You could always count on him for a service project or whatever. I was his Scoutmaster. Never had to push that boy to get his eagle. He planned it all on his own.

"The girl he married always seemed a good enough girl, but she was kind of uppity. She was real pretty, and she knew it. She was the kind that always had to stand out in a crowd, be praised and pampered. I think he's done a good job this time in choosing. I like you, missy. You put up with me and my mess awful good. That says something about a person. I'd about expected you to throw your hands in the air and quit as soon as you saw it. Ruthie, she used to do it quite often. But you stuck with it, even though I know you're not feeling good. You're a good girl."

"Thank you, Mr. Shaw."

"It's Lou. Now go home and take care of yourself. And, if you're sick tomorrow, just call and don't worry about com'in in. You hear?"

"I hear. Thanks, Lou. And, call me Jana." She smiled despite how she was feeling. "I'll see you tomorrow."

Maggie sent her to her room the minute she walked through the door. Jana hardly remembered climbing under the covers. The next thing she knew, Ty was calling her for dinner.

"You know, dear, you really don't sound very well. Maybe we should have Doc come over and have a look at you," Maggie suggested during dinner.

"There's no reason to bother him, I'll be fine with a little rest."

"I probably would have something for you." Maggie offered.

"No, that's okay. I don't think I'm much into taking things. That cough medicine you gave me earlier is fine. I'll take some more right before I go to bed."

"After dinner, Dad and I are going to watch a movie,"

Tyler spoke up. "It's a whodunit. Want to join us?"

"Sure," Jana agreed.

"The challenge is to figure it out before Dad," Ty informed her.

"Is he good?"

"Yeah, I guess that's why he's the sheriff."

"That sounds like he has an unfair advantage, if you ask me." She looked at JT.

"Unfair!" JT returned, mock outrage colored his voice. "I'll tell you what, I'll solve tonight's mystery within the first fifteen minutes and if I can't do it, I'll treat everyone to ice cream at Johnson's."

"Waffle cones?" Jana added.

"You're as bad as Ty. Waffle cones," he agreed, sticking out his hand.

"You're on." She stuck out her hand. Instead of shaking it, JT gave a tug, pulling her up against him.

"I say we seal it with a kiss." He added another challenge, in a low husky voice.

"I have a cold." She squeaked out a warning.

"I'll chance it." He kissed her quick and hard. She was speechless when he raised his head and looked to his son. "I think that sealed the bargain, don't you?"

Tyler grinned and nodded, his eyes twinkling with delight. JT hoped the twinkle in Jana's eyes was from a wave of passion that matched the one that coursed through his body.

With dinner over, they moved in front of the TV.

"How about I get the dessert and bring it in here?" Jana volunteered.

"Sounds good. Need a hand?" JT asked.

"Nope, just get comfortable. But, don't start without me!"

JT didn't need any other encouragement. Settling down on the couch, he stretched his feet out in front of him and placed his hands behind his head with an exaggerated sigh. "Man, is life good. A beautiful woman waiting on me and a full fifteen minutes to solve a mystery. It's a done deal. What could be better?"

Ty and Jana exchanged looks.

"He is so going down." She winked and headed for the kitchen.

"Yeah," Ty settled on the floor. "Hurry, Jana."

Jana did quicken her pace, happiness coursing through her body. Her heart gave a lurch that JT thought she was beautiful. She definitely didn't feel like a plain Jane around him. No, here she felt special. She knew this was what she'd been looking for in life. She fairly danced into the kitchen.

"You seem to be feeling better," Maggie said her as she placed a dish in the dishwasher.

"I am." Jana picked up several dishes from the table.

"Don't worry about these. You better hurry." The older woman shooed her away.

"It'll just take a second to help you."

"You just scoop up the ice cream. I've got this all but finished."

Jana took a scoop out of the drawer. She put ice cream in the bowls and then stacked a dozen cookies on a plate.

"Jana," Ty yelled from the other room.

"Coming," Jana called out, picking up the tray. Pushing the door open with her hip, she said loudly. "How about ice cream, just in case our illustrious sheriff can't …"

Her voice trailed off as she caught sight of the TV screen and the shadowed hand holding a knife, striking out. No air would enter her lungs as the man in the movie dropped to the floor, the knife still lodge in his blood-soaked chest.

○ვ৪ე

JT jerked around as the tray hit the floor, his eyes going from the TV to Jana.

She stood still, a statue modeled in terror. Eyes wide, mouth open in a soundless scream. Fear blatantly etched on her face.

"Jana," JT said softly, carefully getting to his feet. He sensed any sudden movement would send her fleeing.

"No," she whispered over and over again, taking steps backward with every word. Her face still locked on the TV, but JT doubted she was really seeing it.

Everything burst all at once. Maggie pushed open the kitchen door bustling in. "What happened?"

The sudden noise set Jana off. She screamed and flew for the door and outside.

JT sprang after her, but terror gave her extra momentum.

The night was cold, crisp and clear. A nearly full moon lit the yard, making it easy to see Jana as she ran as if for her life. JT took off after her, but his longer strides were making little head way. Calling her name was no help. In her terror, she seemed totally oblivious to him. She darted round rocks and bushes, heading for the grove of trees down by the creek.

Cʒꙶ

Jana's heart pumped, pushing her on, away from the blood, away from the knife. Snarling figures reached out, tearing at her clothes, tripping up her feet. She fell once tumbling down an incline. She hit hard but didn't let it slow her. Spurred on by the heavy sound of footsteps in pursuit, she scrambled to her feet and was off again.

The demon after her called her name, but she refused to relent. Struggling on, her strength failed and she fell again. Unable to go any further, she pressed into a hiding place and prayed she wouldn't be found. But the rustling came closer and closer until she couldn't take it any longer. Bursting from her hiding place, she tumbled into the icy water of the creek that swallowed her whole.

Cʒꙶ

JT couldn't believe that Jana could keep up the pace she was running. He wasn't sure he could. His lungs burned from the cold air. He surged forward when he saw her fall, hoping to catch her as she slid down the embankment.

Her impact with a tree hardly slowed her. His descent was more cautious, and for a moment he was afraid he'd lost her. Then her coughing brought on by cold air and her running came as a beacon leading him through the trees.

He heard her give a small shriek and guessed she'd fallen again. Unable to see her, he slowed and listened. First he only heard the creek at the bottom of the hill, then he could hear her coughs, muffled he guessed by her hand. He knew he was getting closer when he could hear the soft whimpering sound she made.

"Quiet, have to be … quiet." The hushed sound was punctuated by her coughing spells.

JT stopped moving, knowing he was close but not wanting to scare her further. "Jana," he said softly. "Jana, it's me, JT. Jana sweetheart, it's all right." He took a couple steps toward her.

She burst out of the bush. Her frantic flight took her right into the cold, snow-fed, water of the creek.

JT reached the creek on a run, fighting for his balance as the creek bottom turned under his stocking-clad feet. He caught Jana by her shirt. She came out of the water fighting, but what little strength she had left was sapped by the cold water. She went limp in his arms, shivering, coughing and sobbing.

Cradling her to him, he carried her out of the water. Repeating her name softly, he staggered up the bank trying to force his body heat into her. The only trouble was, he figured the cold had chilled his body to the point there wasn't much heat to give. Climbing the slope was more difficult than coming down though she had become still in his arms.

It didn't matter there was little light to see his footing,

since he couldn't see them over Jana anyway. Each step, he had to feel his way then test it before he shifted his weight. He fell once, going to his knees, but managed to keep her tucked tight to his chest.

Jana no longer tried to escape, but a new set of whimpers slipped from her bringing on another siege of coughing. JT kept a running commentary of soothing words. It wasn't until they reached the top, and he started across the meadow that he had any sign she was back with him.

"JT," she whispered his name. After the next set of deep, pain-filled coughs eased, she whispered his name again stronger, pressing her face into his neck. Her arms wrapped tight around his shoulders making it easier to hold her.

All the lights were on in the yard to greet them. Maggie and Ty stepped out on the porch as soon as he approached.

"Run, turn on my shower. She fell in the creek," JT yelled and Maggie disappeared back into the house, while Tyler raced to him.

"We already called Dr. Phillips. Is she all right Dad?" Ty asked scampering at his heals like a little puppy.

"She will be. She's just cold."

"What happened?"

JT knew the question would be coming from his son. He'd been thinking it himself. He just didn't have an answer. "We'll talk about it later. Can you get the door, son?"

Ty ran ahead, holding it open.

Walking through the room down the hall, JT went straight to the shower. Stepping in, not bothering with his own clothes. The water was blessedly warm on his skin. JT could only imagine how it was for her. He let her feet slide to the floor, still balancing her with his body.

Jana sighed and slumped against him, only disturbed

by sporadic fits of coughing that ripped through her.

"Doc's here," Maggie said in the doorway. Moving out of the shower, he accepted the towel Maggie held out for him and started wiping down Jana's face and hair.

"Jana, sweetheart, we have to get you out of your wet clothes. I want you to sit here." He directed her down on the commode. He knelt down and slipped her shoes off her feet then socks. He looked up to Maggie, "Can you handle the rest, and I'll get out of my wet things."

"We'll be fine. Just sit with her while I get her something to change into." Maggie disappeared, returning a minute later.

JT left them with one more glance back. Torn between the need to give her privacy and the desire to be with her, he backed from the room.

"JT." The sound of Jana calling his name almost did him in.

"I'm right here, sweetheart." The endearment slipped out naturally. "Get changed and I'll be right back to carry you to bed."

Obediently, Jana raised her hands to her buttons to comply but found her finger too shaky to work the small disks through the holes.

"Here let me help." Maggie said.

JT stepped into the closet, quickly changed, then waited and listened until it sounded like they were finished before he came out. "You look better."

Jana tried to smile, but it came out weak. She made it to her feet and held out her arms to him.

JT caught her, holding her a minute before he swept her up.

She snuggled against him, rubbing her cheek against his shoulder like a little kitten. Her eyelids drooped before he had taken a few steps, then a round of coughing disturbed her.

JT was tempted to just put her in his bed, but he was

already becoming too tempted by her and decided, that though as innocent as it was, it wasn't a smart idea so headed to hers.

He'd just made it to her room when Doc stepped into the hall. "Missy, it seems like we keep meeting like this," he teased, trying to coax a smile from her. "That sounds like a nasty cough you have."

JT lowered her to the bed. He wanted to remain holding her. He also wanted to ask her what had frightened her so much that she ran like that, but as Doc took out his stethoscope, he stepped back.

Doc listened to her heart and lungs then checked her ears and throat.

When he finished, Jana sagged limply against her pillow.

"I want you to take this." He handed her a pill then the glass of water Maggie had brought in. He nodded satisfied after she had taken it. "That should help you sleep more comfortably. Close your eyes now."

Closing her eyes was the last thing Jana wanted to do, afraid the horrible images would come back.

Maggie and Doc had already turned to leave the room. JT hesitated. The scowl on his face was quite daunting. But, when he turned to go, Jana knew she didn't want him to leave her. She was afraid and needed him like she had never needed anyone before.

"JT." His name trembled past her lips, but it was enough to stop him. The scowl was gone when he turned back, replaced with concern and love. Warmth flowed over Jana.

He crossed the room to her in a single long stride. Settling on the bed, he reached for her, pulling her into his arms where Jana longed to be.

Again his name was the only thing she was able to get out before tears fell.

"Shh, sweetheart. I have you." He rubbed her back

while she cried. After a minute, he probed. "Would you like to talk about it?"

She shook her head even as the words started to tumble out. "It was my nightmare. I was running. The image of the knife … the blood. I just couldn't get away from it."

Her tears soaked his shirt, but he didn't complain. Silently, he settled back against the headboard and tucked the blanket tighter around her. He held her to him with one hand, while he stroked her damp hair with the other.

"I need a brush." She managed a big sniff.

"I'll get it." JT acted immediately, easing her up to pull away. When a small sound of objection slipped from her, he comforted. "I'll be right back." He stood and picked up the brush on the dresser and returned to the bed. Leaning her against him once more, he started to work the brush through her damp locks.

Jana felt her eyes start to drift close, then jerked them open.

"Shh," JT consoled.

"I don't want to fall asleep." It took effort for her to force the words out.

"It's all right. I'll be near." He brushed his lips against her temple and continued to run the brush through her hair. She loved the feel. Her eyes drifted shut, as she listened to the comforting beat of his heart.

JT knew she was asleep. What he didn't know was the reason behind her fears. He didn't like the explanations his mind was coming up with. Her terror was so real. He knew he had to figure out what was causing it so he could help her. He had to help her. It was no longer a duty. It was personal.

Her hair dry, he sat the brush on the nightstand and continued to run his fingers through the silky strands. He was going over things in his mind when he became aware of Ty in the doorway.

"Is she okay?" his son asked in a hushed voice, worry

159

showing in his eyes.

"She's sleeping." JT motioned him in. Ty hesitated slightly before coming over and settling on the edge of the bed by him.

"What happened?"

"I've been trying to figure that out. As near as I can figure ..." he paused to collect his thoughts. "Jana's been having nightmares. It seems that the picture on the TV triggered the nightmare. It became real to her and she ran."

"You don't think she saw someone stabbed, then."

JT almost smiled at the boy's imagination, then thought about it.

"I think that it would be highly unlikely. Things like that don't happen very often. And for you to see something like that, you would have to be pretty close. Killers usually don't make a mistake like killing someone in front of a witness. Unfortunately for police, it usually doesn't happen that handy."

Ty was quiet for a minute. JT could almost see the thoughts turning in his mind, but when he spoke his question, it surprised him.

"Dad, do you think Jana will stay? I want her to." The boy hurried on. "You want her to, I know you do."

"You're right, I've been thinking on that, but she hasn't been here long, and without her memory, do we really know her."

"We do know her. This is who she is," Ty objected firmly.

JT had to smile at that, but he also had another point he had to make. "Maybe, but she has a whole different life somewhere else. It might be that she'll want it back."

"If she doesn't, will you ask her to stay? She's supposed to be with us. I know she is."

JT was surprised by the fervency in his words. "You know we can't just ask her to stay with us."

"We could if you get married."

"That would be okay with you?"

"Yes."

JT nodded. "So you know, I've thought about it too. And I feel good about it. I didn't want to be attracted to her. I didn't want a woman in our lives. I was just happy having you. I didn't think we needed anyone else in our lives."

"Yes, we do. I know Maggie takes care of us, but I'd like Jana to be here, too."

He had to agree with that. He wanted Jana to be there.

"You understand that we need to give her time. She's been through a lot. We need to make sure she's certain about wanting us."

"Jana likes being here," Ty said with certainty.

"I think you're right, but we still don't know what she left behind." He didn't want to say it, but he had to. "She might have someone that she loves there and is already planning to get married to." It tore him to think of her loving someone else.

"No, they'd be looking for her," Ty stated JT's own thoughts.

"Again, you're right, but we'll have to give her time to know for sure. For now though, why don't you head for bed? You have school tomorrow."

"You're going to stay with Jana?" There was concern in his voice for the woman who had come into their lives.

"For a little while, until I'm sure she's okay."

As Ty left, JT moved to a chair beside the bed. He sat longer then he planned, but thoughts of her kept him awake and sitting there. Sometime during the night, he drifted off to sleep because, when he came alert, the house was quiet and dark but for a light in the hall bathroom.

Jana lay snuggled peacefully in bed. Again, the feeling of rightness disturbed him a little, but he was beginning to accept it. His mind started to drift off when something else disturbed him. JT couldn't say what it was, but something was wrong.

Standing, he glanced down at Jana, watching as she shifted in her sleep, almost like she was reaching out to him. He started to smile then turned to the door. He walked through the dark, silent house, checking all the doors and windows. Nothing seemed amiss. At the back porch, he paused, unsure why, he pulled on his work boots and denim jacket.

The air outside was crisp and chilling against his sleep warmed skin, making him think of returning to the house. Instead, he moved on. Cool air was good for him. It cleared his mind. He hadn't been this hot and bothered since he was a teen.

Pushing the barn door open, he stepped inside. The only thing that changed in the barn was the status in Daisy's stall. A little colt stood on wobbly legs by his mother. Daisy nickered her greeting as JT slid his hand over her. "Well, look at this. You okay, girl?" As before, Daisy took motherhood in stride.

"Hello there little guy." JT extended his hand out to the velvety nose.

The colt jerked back and made what could only be called a hopping movement.

"Frisky little stinker, isn't he. Ty and Jana will get a kick out of him." His mind was already putting them together as a family.

After a few moments of coaxing, JT was allowed to run his hand over the silky coat. "You did good, Daisy." He scratched the mare's neck one last time before heading in.

ଔଛ

Kellerman pulled back into the shadows, watching the sheriff head back to the house. He had enough of this waiting. He didn't care what Ferrell said. He might not be able to get to her tonight with the good-old-boy sheriff on guard, but tomorrow, no more waiting. Tomorrow, he'd get her. Tomorrow.

Chapter Thirteen

JT had just started down the hall when he heard the first whimper. By the time he made it to Jana's room, the whimpers changed to small meowing cries as Jana twisted and fought with the blanket.

"Jana." His touch on her arm had her flinching away and striking out. A cry ripped from her lips with terror.

"Jana." This time he caught her flailing arms, giving her a soft shake to bring her awake.

Reality came to her in mid cry. The ghastly images disappeared into the familiar shape of JT. With an agonized cry, she threw herself into his arms.

"Oh baby." He caught her to him.

"They're dead. They're all dead," she cried into his chest. Her words shocked him.

"Who's dead?" He forced himself to ask.

"I don't know. I just keep seeing them, the man with the knife and all the blood."

"From the TV." He felt a moment of relief until she answered again.

"No, no. The man in my dreams. And the other man, he has a gun in his hand, and he's yelling at me. Blood is spreading down his arm and side."

JT felt his throat tightening. "Jana, what man with a gun?"

"The one on the ground, yelling at me. The woman has a gun too, but everything explodes and she's gone." Jana was crying harder now. "They're dead." She repeated it over and over again. "I wish the images would go away, but it's like I have to remember them." Her coughing returned, and she could no longer get words out.

When he finally got her settled and her crying slowed, he gave her the medicine Doc left. Closing her eyes, she slumped back into the pillow, her breathing labored. She was just starting to ease when she shot up in bed. "I have to leave."

"What?" JT was caught off guard.

"I have to leave. People die around me." She slid off the bed and wobbled as she stood, but it didn't slow her from grabbing up her bag off the closet floor.

"Jana, what are you doing?"

She swayed on her feet.

He barely caught her before she smashed into the wall. A feeling of loss stabbed through him at the thought of her leaving him.

"I've got to go." She was crying when she turned to look at him. Agony etched her face. "I can't let anything happened to you or Ty. I think I'm a bad person."

JT stared in disbelief at the woman in front of him. He might not know all about her but he did trust his impression of her, and she was a good person. He couldn't feel what he did for her if she wasn't. The idea was ludicrous, but it was evident she didn't think so.

Tears streaked down her face. Pain filled her blue eyes. Her gently curved body trembled. It was obvious her legs were ready to buckle under her. She was sweet, fragile and beautiful. If she wasn't so serious about thinking she was a bad person, he would've laughed.

"Jana." He started forward.

"No," she cried out, backing away.

"You're not bad."

"You don't know that."

"I do. Inside me, I know."

She shook her head. "I keep seeing things over and

over again. They're real." Agony dropped her voice to a whisper. "They're real."

"They're nightmares."

Again her head shook. "No … No."

"Yes." He reached for her other hand and drew her to him before she could object.

She fought to break away. "Let me go. I have to go."

He felt the strength leaving her body. "Where would you go?"

"Away. Anywhere, so you'll be safe."

"No. Shh." He stroked her back, reveling in the feel of holding her. "You're staying here."

"No."

"Yes."

"No, I can't. I can't." The sobs racked her body. "What about Ty? What about Maggie? If anything happened to Ty, I'd die."

"Nothing is going to happen to Tyler."

"What if I hurt you?" She was losing all rationality now. She was so panicked, JT was afraid she was going into shock.

"Shh, Jana. Nothing is going to happen to me, Ty or Maggie. You're not going to hurt anyone. You couldn't." He was positive of what he said. "The only way you could hurt me is if you leave."

She started shaking her head. "No, you don't know that."

"I do. I know you."

"No," she said, but she was weakening.

"You'd never hurt anyone. You're too caring. That's one of the things I love about you."

"No." She pulled back trying to tug away from his hold, but her strength failed her.

"Yes. I know you, Jana. I'd bet my badge on what kind of woman you are. You are not bad. Trust me on this."

Her crying was soft now, and she leaned limply against

his body. Sliding one hand down her back, he lifted her into his arms and carried her to bed, tucking the covers around her. Leaning over, he pressed kisses over her forehead and down her cheek.

The thought of her excited him, but this was not the time to get those thoughts. So he cuddled her tight giving her his comfort and assurance until once more she fell asleep. This time he resolved to remain at her side as a guardian to keep the nightmares at bay.

JT didn't wake until he heard Tyler in the hall. He disengaged himself from the chair, moving stiffly as he made his way to the kitchen. "Morning," he greeted his son and aunt.

"How's Jana?" Maggie greeted back.

"She had a rough night but seems to be sleeping now. Just let her sleep."

Maggie nodded. "You're heading into town?"

"Yeah." He had some digging to do, and he wasn't going to stop until he found some answers. Jana couldn't handle any more of this not knowing. "Listen, would you call me when she wakes up and let me know how she's doing?"

⟡

Jana came awake slowly. The room was warm. The blinds on the window only let slits of light in. She didn't need the clock to tell her she had slept late, but was surprised when she read ten thirty-four.

The nightmare of last night came back with surprising clarity, bringing with it a strong feeling of uncertainty. Turning her head on the pillow, she was greeted by JT's masculine scent. It was a smell that held comfort and rightness for her.

He'd held her there and soothed away the terrors. He was a good man. She felt a blast of longing and love. But after last night, she wondered if she would ever be able to have him in her life.

For now, she would put her trust in JT. He wouldn't let her down. It would be all right. She had to believe that, just as she had to believe she was not a bad person.

Maggie was starting a load of laundry when Jana stepped into the kitchen, finally ready to start the day.

"Good morning," Maggie's greeting came from the laundry room.

"It's almost afternoon," Jana answered sheepishly.

"Well, you needed the sleep." The older woman started the washer then joined her in the kitchen. "Now sit down here and let's get you something to eat. Your voice sounds better. How's the cough?"

Until that moment, Jana hadn't even thought about it. "Gone, I feel much better." Then it dawned on her she was supposed to be at work. "I have to call Mr. Shaw."

"I already called Lou. He said for you to rest and come in when you felt up to it," Maggie said.

"Thank you so much. I wouldn't want him to think that now I got my car back I wouldn't hold up my end of the bargain."

"I don't think that thought ever entered his mind."

"Well, I'd better get going."

"Huh-uh, girl. You're going to sit right down here. You're not going anywhere until you eat something good and healthy. I have some homemade chicken noodle soup I fixed up this morning. It's awful good, if I do say so myself."

"Mmm, homemade noodles," Jana savored the taste a few minutes later and finished two bowls before heading to Lou's garage.

⟶⟵

JT was becoming frustrated when nothing came from his early morning calls. He decided it was time to call in every old marker he had. When the first several of those were dead ends, he called a friend in the FBI who was assigned to the Denver office. He had tried Malcolm on

Friday, but he had been out of the office. This time JT lucked out, and he was put right through. "Agent Bryant," the voice said on the line.

"Malcolm, it's about time you went to work," JT greeted teasingly. "You ever going to lay off the lady chasing and get some work done?"

Malcolm Bryant could have been his twin, but he had dark hair and eyes. They had the same build, same movement patterns, and the same type of chiseled features. Even their personalities had an uncanny resemblance.

"JT, what are you up to? Finally got some real crime in that little community of yours and want the big boys to come in and handle it?"

"Yeah, right. Actually, I am calling for a favor. I have a license plate that I've been trying to run, and I'm having a beast of a time getting anything. I was wondering if you could ask some questions for me."

"Sure, but what's so all-fired important?"

"You won't believe this, but I have a woman with amnesia."

"Amnesia? You're pulling my leg." Malcolm laughed.

"Nope, totally serious." He went on to explain about what had been happening. "I need some answers for her. She's had all she can take of not knowing anything."

"Do I detect something more here?"

JT was surprised that his friend picked up on his interest and didn't hesitate to answer. "Yeah, you do. I've fallen in love with her."

"Are you sure you're not pulling my leg. I mean, like … I know you and what about Ty."

"It's definitely okay with him. The two get along together like wildfire. I think it's going to be okay, and if it is, I'm going to marry her."

"I didn't think I'd ever hear you say that after, well …" He let it hang.

"You haven't met Jana yet."

"All right, give me the info, and I'll get back as soon as I can."

"Thanks, you come through, and you can be best man at my wedding."

"I try to stay away from those, but you can name your next kid after me. Talk to you in a couple." At that, he hung up.

ᴄʒᴏ

The non-descript sedan pulled up to the garage. The watcher first caught a glimpse of white tennis shoes then the jean clad legs, before the woman he had been waiting for came into view. She had finally shown up. He was beginning to think he'd have to come up with another plan.

Now it was time to prepare. First, he needed to steal a car, but in this trusting type of town, that wouldn't be hard. She'd be there for several hours so he had time to do it, really careful.

ᴄʒᴏ

JT stood, trying to decide about walking over to the garage to see Jana. Maggie had called when she had left the house, and he had watched her car drive by earlier. He was relieved that her thoughts of leaving didn't seem to be around today. He was almost to the door when his phone rang.

"Sheriff's office."

"JT."

"Malcolm, you got some news for me?" he said in the way of greeting, recognizing the voice.

"Do I ever?"

JT's chest tightened at Malcolm's words. "What is it?"

"Well, the reason you were having so much trouble tracing the car is it's a cover car. I'll tell you, it took some digging and a couple of favors to the U.S. Marshal's. The car is theirs. It was assigned to a marshal protecting a witness who was killed last week in an explosion, an assassination. Anyway, the marshal's been listed as missing since. They think she was the one that gave the tip. A large amount of money appeared in her bank account the day after."

JT turned colder with each word. "Why in the heck didn't I get a reaction when I first ran the car?"

"Things there were pretty much in turmoil on the case. One marshal was shot several times. He's still in critical condition. The only witness to a murder-fraud case on a man they want really bad, was blown up. Another marshal is missing. It wasn't until two days later they turned up the evidence.

"Anyway, her name is Karen Richmond, age twenty eight," Malcolm started to continue with the statistics, but JT cut him off.

"Wait a minute. That's not right. Her name is Jana."

"Sorry, JT, Jana Hamilton was killed when the safe house exploded. She was the witness."

"That can't be." His heart hurt.

"I'm afraid it is. Jana Hamilton is dead. Karen Richmond was an abandoned child. Put herself through college, then went right to the Marshals. She's a loner, twenty eight, five-five, green eyes, reddish brown hair."

"Wait a minute. Wait. Green eyes, reddish brown hair, that's not her."

"Are you sure? Maybe she changed her hair."

"Believe me, she could change her hair, but I know her eyes."

"Contacts?"

"No! But an explosion fits a couple of injures she had when she showed up. Listen, let me fax you her pictures, so you can see."

"All right. Give me a minute to go to the fax room, and pick it up, and I'll call you right back."

Two minutes later the phone rang. JT picked it up and Malcolm started talking, not waiting for the greeting. "You have the supposedly dead witness. Jana Hamilton, twenty-five, junior accountant that saw her boss murdered by one Cameron Kellerman. Authorities have been after him a long time. She walked in on the murder. They don't have the murder weapon so, without her, there's no case. They thought they'd lost her. We're running a check on Kellerman now."

"You mean he's not in jail," JT rasped.

"No, he made the million dollar bail."

JT almost broke his rules about not swearing. "If Kellerman knows she's not dead, then he's had almost two weeks to find her."

"Right, I got my supervisor here now and though it's not our case, since a bomb was used, I've been cleared to come. We're contacting the Marshals, and I'm on my way. Just sit on her until we get there. That lady is worth a lot. And even more valuable dead to some people."

As soon as the phone dropped to the cradle, JT was running out the door. The blasted nightmares were real.

∞

Jana pushed the creaky chair back from the desk and stretched. Lou's taxes were done. She felt a surge of pride in her accomplishment and decided to go tell Lou the good news. Jana stepped into the work bay just as she saw the man slide around the corner of the garage door. The sun at his back obscured his features, but something about the man sent a chill though her, stopping Jana in midstride.

It wasn't until the man grabbed a wrench from the workbench and stepped behind Lou that Jana was jarred back into motion.

"No," she screamed diving for the man. It was too late to stop the wrench's downward swing, but it was enough to startle the man into missing his mark. The heavy tool grazed off Lou's head connecting with his shoulder before it hit the car, jarring it from Kellerman's hand. Lou slumped forward into the engine.

The man spun to face Jana as she rounded the car.

Memories of his face swamped her. They brought her to the ground as much as the blow from his hand. If the wrench had still been in his hand, it would have killed her. As it was, it left her stunned.

Visions burst back, one after another – the house exploding, Jake shot and bleeding, and running in terror down the hall from the man that stood over her. The man reached down to pull her to her feet. The image mingled with the memories of him standing over Mr. Murdock with the bloody knife in hand.

Jana tried to fight the hand that clamped on her arm, pulling her to the man who was her terror, but her motions were disjointed and ineffective.

"You should have kept your mouth shut. You should have died." He spat into her face. "So much work. So much time. Do you know how much you cost me?" His breath fanned her face. She tried to brush his head away. He caught her wrist easily, twisting it painfully behind her. "Come on." He shoved her through the office door.

"Open the register." When she failed to comply, he jerked her arm higher.

She cried out and tears filled her eyes.

"Open the register." The words ground by her ear. "And take out the money."

Her free hand trembled violently as she pushed the buttons then tried to remove the cash. Just as she pulled it free, he hit her hand, sending the money drifting all over the floor.

"Now let's go." The gun seemed to materialize in his hand. He pressed it into her neck while twisting her arm to force her to the back door. A cry escaped her lips, and she feared her arm would break. Jana knew that was the least of her troubles.

All her past memories of the man flooded back to her. She knew who he was and knew she was dead if he got her out of the garage. He was going to kill her.

Help. She screamed in her mind and the roar of an engine and tires screeching out front answered. Her hope that someone would come dropped into fear with the knowledge that they'd die also.

Giving her no chance to call out, Kellerman pressed the gun deeper into her neck. "Not a word or they die too," he threatened as if reading her mind. He continued to push her toward the back door.

Jana heard her name just as she was shoved into the alley. It was the ache of never hearing JT say her name again, never knowing what it was to love him, never having the opportunity to feel his child move within her that released her will to fight.

She threw herself back against Kellerman, who was looking into the garage. She caught him off-guard, sending him into a pile of discarded tires just outside the door. Jana didn't look back. She ran, dodging between two cars waiting to be repaired. She ducked down and kept moving.

One side of the garage property opened to a vacant lot. Behind that was a horse pasture. Both had no cover so if she ran that way she would be seen easily. The other side led down the alley behind the restaurant and into town. It would give her plenty of opportunities to escape. The only problem was, she was on the opposite side of the yard, and Kellerman was between her and the alley.

Jana froze, listening as she moved and began to make her way from hiding place to hiding place. She feared each move but was more afraid if she stayed in one place, Kellerman would find her.

Dodging around a truck that had its front bashed in, she stumbled over a fourteen inch long piece of metal pipe that was half-buried in the dirt. She didn't know what it was and thought it was a pretty pitiful weapon against a gun, but it was better than nothing. She grabbed it before making her next move.

She had made it about a third of the distance to the

alley when she caught her first glimpse of Kellerman. Fortunately, he was looking the other way. Unfortunately, he was only eight feet away. Jana froze, not daring to move, fearing to even breathe, that he might hear her. Her fears that she would cough returned and were enough to aggravate her subconscious to make her throat tickle.

She forgot about the need to cough when JT came through the door, not only catching her attention, but Kellerman's, who was facing that direction. Kellerman dropped down behind a car and trained his gun on JT.

Chapter Fourteen

The tires squealed as JT came to a stop in front of Lou's. No one was at the pump, but JT didn't feel fear until he saw the register drawer open and money scattered all over the floor.

"Jana, Lou," he called their names as he dashed the few steps into the garage. He immediately saw Lou slumped under the hood of the car he'd been working on. Moving forward in a crouch, he checked the older man and, though he was unconscious, his pulse was strong. The noise he heard out back had him moving cautiously in that direction.

He paused just inside the bay enough to call in for backup and an ambulance. With gun in hand, he was careful as he stepped into the sun. The metal mat at the doorway clanked at his feet. Out of the corner of his eye, he picked up a movement on the left.

JT dodged behind the tires the instant the shot rang out. The bullet missed him only by a fraction of an inch. It embedding harmlessly into the thick rubber of a tire, where his head had been an instant earlier.

"JT," Jana's cry echoed the gun fire. She erupted from close to where the shot had come, wielding a piece of metal like a bat. Unable to see the attacker, JT's heart about stopped as he heard the sound of the gun go off at the same time he saw Jana swing and cry out.

JT flew from his cover, weaving his way toward Jana. He had yet to see who was shooting. The next shot came clanging off metal a good two feet from him.

"Stop right there, Sheriff, or the lady dies."

He would have laughed because it sounded so like a common line from a movie, if it hadn't been for the hard edge of desperation in the voice, and the fact that Jana's life was in the balance. He worked a few feet further, trying to get so he could see her.

"Stop," the man ordered. JT froze, not so much for the command but the sight of the woman he had come to love in just a few short days. Jana was pulled back against the man like a shield, covering all but the few inches where he topped her.

A dirty old ball cap was pulled low over the man's head, but he should have changed the high priced leather loafers, if he'd wanted to convince him that he was a down-on-his-luck gas station robber. The man was there for Jana, and unless he did something, JT knew she was dead. Still, he'd played it the killer's way for the moment, until he could formulate a plan.

"Come on, let the lady go," JT said calmly.

"Don't think so. She's my ticket out'a here." The fakeness in the man's voice was so heavy that, instead of making JT want to laugh, it gave him a stab of fear.

"Robbery is one thing, but you don't want to add kidnapping." JT could hear the sirens and knew his deputies were about there. The man didn't have much time. Jana, who had been quiet up to then, gave a little squeak as the arm tightened on her neck.

"Tell your men to stay back."

When JT didn't move to follow the order, the man with the gun shoved the barrel rougher against her head.

Jana whimpered.

"Tell them!" the man yelled, pressing Jana's head over, letting JT get a good look at his eyes for the first time. Wild was the only way to describe them. This man was not only a cruel killer, but he had lost it. He was insane, which added a whole new slant on the equation.

Not taking his eyes or his gun off the man, JT used his free hand to get his radio. "Pull back, Monty. We have a hostage situation. Gerald, do not pass Ralph's."

He trusted his men enough to know that, in a couple minutes, he'd have a man out front making sure Lou was seen to and another at the end of the alley after making sure every door along it was lock and barred. The man was as cut off, as he could make it.

Now he just had to get Jana out of harm's way. To do that he, needed to clear his thoughts of the fear in her eyes, eyes that seem to say I'm sorry and I love you. He needed to think like a clear headed professional.

C3&

Jana wanted to tell JT how sorry she was for the trouble and pain she had caused and that she loved him. The arm that was wrapped around her neck hardly let enough air in to breathe, leaving no extra air to get a word out. She also wanted to yell at JT to get away, that the man was a killer. She knew it wouldn't do any good to warn him. JT was a lawman and a good man. He wasn't the type of man to leave anyone in trouble.

She could see the tension in JT's body and the wheels turning in his mind. He was waiting, watching and planning. Jana was afraid he would do something to get himself shot more than she was afraid she would be.

She listened to him talk to his deputies and felt Kellerman's body tense. The instant Kellerman shifted, and the arm on her neck loosened slightly, Jana knew he was going to shoot JT. The same time the gun came down from her head toward JT, Jana slammed back with all the force she could into the killer.

The shot that echoed in her ears went wide. Kellerman tried to regain his hold on her, but Jana kicked and fought like a wild cat until she was pushed to the ground. The gun in Kellerman's hand swung directly in her face. Jana flinched at the explosion. Her breath held, waiting for the searing pain or nothingness. A second shot roared, and she felt the bullet pass by her ear, leaving it ringing.

She wondered if her face held the same shocked look as Kellerman's the moment before he crumpled down on top of her. Too stunned to scream or cry, she lay smothered under the lifeless body.

⋅⋅⋅

JT could see the decision in the man's eyes just before he turned the gun to him. Though he trusted his own skills with the gun, he knew the shot would be tricky with Jana in the way. Still he had no choice.

He was about to take the shot when Jana took to fighting. She scratched and kicked. The man, unable to control her, pushed her back. The gun swung toward her.

JT got the impression that Jana had won the fight but was about to lose the war. He fired a split second before the other man. Even as the killer toppled another shot rang out, then the alley was filled with heavy silence.

"Jana." Her name made it across his lips in an agonized whisper as he started forward. He hardly paused to make sure the man was dead before he threw off the body. Blood was smeared over her slacks and shirt. Her eyes showed no signs of seeing him, but the quiver in her chin told him she was alive.

"Jana, where are you hurt?" He started running his hands over her finding no injury. "Jana! Talk to me!" he yelled desperately, still searching.

"He killed … I saw …" she stuttered out.

"I know, baby. I know," he soothed. "Sweetheart, I need you to look at me. I need you to tell me where you're hurt. That's it," he urged, when her gaze drifted to him. As soon her eyes rested on him, they widened. He had no time to steady himself when she launched herself into his chest.

His arms automatically went around her, only too happy to hold her. He basked in the feel of her clinging to him. Her nose pressed into his neck. He felt her tears and quivering. He hated to pull away, but there were things that needed to be done. The first was to assure himself that she wasn't injured and then to call his men and let them know the situation.

"Jana," he eased her back. "Sweetheart, it's okay. I have you, but I need you to tell me where you're hurt."

"I … I'm all right." Tears streamed down her face. "I saw him. He stabbed my boss. I saw him."

"Shh, it's over now. Shh."

"Lou! He killed Lou." Her cry rang with pain.

"No." JT gripped her head, forcing her to look at him so she could see the truth in his face. "Lou is not dead. He'll be okay. My deputies are with him. He'll be okay, understand me?"

She nodded, and he could see her pulling herself back together.

"That's my girl." He smiled and she returned it with a weak one. "I need to talk to my men now. You okay?"

"Yes." She glanced over at the dead man then back to him. "Yes, I'm okay."

Again, a smile made it to his lips as he looked at her. He had just shot a man. She had almost been killed and was covered in blood, but she was all right.

Things got busy after he radioed his deputies. Gerald came running down the alley. With the coast clear, Monty let the ambulance in to take care of Lou, who he reported was coming around.

Jana made the ID on the body. JT drew her near as she said the name, Cameron Kellerman. She said she remembered everything. That she had seen him kill her boss, and he had tried to kill her. The tears that slid down her face left him torn between the need to comfort her and the job he needed to do with the crime scene.

He kept her close until Doc and Maggie arrived to take her to the hospital to be checked out. They brought news with them that Lou was going to be fine. He had regained full consciousness and was already trying to get out of the hospital.

JT didn't see Jana again until several hours later, at home, where Maggie had taken her. She was asleep on her bed, wrapped in his robe. Her freshly washed hair was fanned out around her. She looked sweet and peaceful.

He wondered, now she had her memory back, how things would be for her. He feared he might lose her and then shook the thought off. He wasn't going to give up now. He wasn't going to give up ever. She was in his life, and he was going to fight to keep her there.

He reached out to touch her cheek then stopped his hand just an inch short. He didn't want to wake her. Besides, she wasn't his yet. He looked at his outstretched hand and wondered if it was an indication she was untouchable and would always be out of his reach. *No!* But he flexed his fingers a second before he let his hand drop to his side. He was almost to the door when he heard her say his name.

"JT." Her voice was soft but enough to pull him back around. He was greeted by a loving, sleepy smile. It warmed him like nothing could.

"I didn't mean to wake you." His body moved to her on its own accord. When her arms lifted, he settled down, slid his own around her, hugging her close.

"I'm glad you're here." She had a dreamy quality about her as she cuddled to him. She rubbed her cheek against his chest in that kitten-type of way. He reciprocated by stroking his hand down her hair and back.

"How are you?" He dipped his chin to kiss her forehead, reveling in the feel of her safe in his arms.

"Sleepy." She stifled a yawn against his chest. "Doc gave me something. I can't stay awake."

"That's good."

"I'm still glad you're here. I can ..." she yawned

again, "… remember everything. My family, my job, I remember it all. He was going to kill me."

JT slid a hand up to her cheek, tilting her head until he could look her in the eyes. "He can't hurt you ever again. You don't have to be afraid." He sealed his words with a kiss before tucking her back under his chin. "Just go to sleep now. There are some people here who want to talk to you. But they can wait until after you've had some rest."

"Who's here?"

"U.S. Marshals and a friend of mine from the FBI, but don't worry, they have enough to keep them busy for a while."

"Good. I'm so tired."

"Then go to sleep." She made a little sound in her throat that was almost like a purr. "JT, will you stay here?" She rose up slightly.

"I'll be real close if you need me." He pressed her back down and continued to brush back her hair as she drifted to sleep.

It was getting dark when Jana finally awoke. With her memory back, her whole world seem to change, except for the love she felt for JT and the comfortable feeling that she was truly home. Pulling on her jeans and her *I found myself in Wyoming* T-shirt, she made her way down the hall, directed by the voices coming from the dining room.

"Jana," Tyler called out to her as she passed the family room, and the boy ran to give her a hug. "I heard what happened." Ty's voice rang with excitement. "Dad said you were all right. He's a hero. Though he didn't say that, I heard the other people talking."

"He saved my life," she affirmed, keeping her arms around the boy. "Have you heard how Mr. Shaw is?"

"Yeah, they released him from the hospital. He had a mild concussion, but he's okay."

"I'm glad. It sounds like everyone is in the dining room."

"Yeah, Malcolm is one of Dad's friends with the FBI. He's here and three people from the U.S. Marshals. They've been piecing things together. The guy had followed you. He's been registered at the hotel under an alias for almost a week. Dad figures he stole the truck that ran us off the road. They said he was foolish not to hire someone to come after you, but guessed he had become fanatical with the need to get rid of you. They say, as he saw it, that if you were gone, they couldn't touch him and he'd get away free and clear and then he would probably have left the country."

"It sounds like you've been eavesdropping." JT's deep voice came from the kitchen doorway, startling them.

Ty shuffled a little but didn't look very repentant.

Jana put her arm over Ty's shoulder and gave him a squeeze. "I have to have someone keeping me informed. You know how I forget things," she teased.

That jarred Tyler into another line of thought. "That's right," he burst. "Dad said you have your memories back."

"Yes." She nodded with a smile.

"You remember everything?"

"Pretty much, I think."

"Then you're not married or anything?"

"Ty." JT's warning cut the boy off.

"It's okay. I'm not married, nor have I ever been." She smiled down. "My parents are both gone. I have an older brother who is a civil engineer. He works on power plants all over the world, building or redesigning them to be more efficient. I'm an accountant. I don't have a boyfriend. I have lots of friends, play a lot of sports, but I guess you'd say I'm kind of a normal, boring person. That is, I was until …" She looked at JT and shrugged her shoulders. "You know, all this."

JT nodded, a smile tilted the corner of his lips. "Speaking of which, you have some people waiting to talk to you."

Jana gave Ty's shoulder another squeeze then followed JT to the dining room.

The three men and one woman in the room stood as she entered. JT made introductions first with his friend, Malcolm Bryant with the FBI, and then the Marshals, Pete Ferrell, Judy Hart and Sam Nelson.

"Miss Hamilton, it is nice to meet you." Sam was the first to speak.

Jana reached out to take the hand of the man with silver-tipped hair. She then turned to Pete Ferrell. "I think we've met before."

"No, I don't think I've had the pleasure," Pete Ferrell answered back and shook her hand before the older man directed her to the chair. "We had you down as dead."

"Karen was killed." It was part statement and part question.

"Yes."

Sadness swept over her, making her voice crack. "And Jake?"

"He's still in intensive care in critical condition. He did wake up two days ago but is heavily sedated. They're still not sure, but it's looking up."

Tears broke free and trickled down her cheeks. "I left him. He told me to go, but ..."

"It's all right. Miss Hamilton, we need you to tell us everything that happened. Please give as much detail as you remember," Sam, obviously the ranking man, instructed while everyone else remained quiet when she began to talk.

Several times her voice cracked and tears slipped free. More than anything, JT wanted to go to her and wrap his arms around her and comfort her, but he didn't dare break her concentration as she told what happened. He sat still as tears etched their way down her cheeks and his heart.

Multiple times they had her repeat her story going over every detail, until they were finally satisfied they had gotten every bit of information they possibly could. When the questions seemed to stop coming, Jana sagged in her seat, drained of all energy. She couldn't figure out what she might have given them since she didn't see the shooter.

There had only been one break and that was when Maggie had bustled in with a tray of food, after Jana ended going through the story the first time. Maggie insisted Jana needed to have something to eat before they continued. It had helped her immensely, but it was JT sitting quietly in the corner that got her through.

She glanced at the clock. It was only about twelve. As tired as she was, she would've guessed it was near morning. The hand that came down on her shoulder was gentle in its massaging motion. She sighed, tipping her head back to look up at JT and managed a weak smile.

He leaned down and kissed her forehead. "You need to go to bed." He caught her arm and helped her up. Jana was surprised to see the other people had left the room. She could hear their voices in the entry. "You go on." JT turned away. Jana wanted to call him back, but instead, made her way to her room.

She was just stepping into the bathroom when she saw JT head down the hall toward his room. He stopped a good four feet from her and shifted, as if he needed to ease some of the same tension that Jana felt. She wanted to go to him, to have him comfort her as he had before, but there was a remoteness about him. When she braved a couple steps his direction, he slid slightly to the side.

"You should get some sleep. It's been a trying day for you." His words seemed forced. "You had a lot of memories to deal with."

When he still didn't move to her, Jana wanted to cry. *Yes, I need you to make it better.*

There was silence in the house as they continued to stand and stare at each other.

JT was the first to break the silence. "Goodnight." He moved toward his room, but at the last moment shifted in front of her. His hands came up on both sides of her face. His head swooped down and his lips took hers by storm. Tension burned from his body, scorching her then, before she could register what was happening, he was gone.

His bedroom door closed firmly behind him, leaving her standing totally stunned. Never in her life had she been kissed like that. Having her memories back, she knew that for certain. She also knew she never wanted another man to kiss her like that. There was only one man for her and that man was Jackson Thomas Termaine.

CallBD

Inside his room, JT tried to catch his breath. Forcing himself away from the door, he paced, fighting the demand to go back and take Jana in his arms and kiss her again. He wanted to stake his claim, ask her to marry him, but he couldn't, not before she had time to sort out her life, and come to terms with who she was.

He was afraid, after all the things she had been though, that maybe she wouldn't want any reminders, especially him, in her life. He cringed, thinking about every painful memory she had uttered tonight. They had torn into him. He could only imagine what they'd been like for her. What he felt could not be even a tenth of what it must've been like for her living through it, the terror that she had faced. He shook his head as the revelation sank in a bit more. There was a possibility that what she felt for him wasn't love but the need for comfort and safety.

His first instinct was to ignore the thought, but he knew he couldn't. He'd married a woman who didn't love him, who had essentially used him as means to get what she wanted. He knew Jana wouldn't consciously do that, but he had to give her time to get things sorted out. He just hoped, when she had time, she would decide she still loved him and wanted to spend her life with him.

CallBD

Though exhausted, sleep seemed impossible to Jana,

she longed to seek JT out and ask what was wrong but couldn't bring herself to leave her room. She wished for understanding, but like sleep, it wasn't forthcoming. Sometime before dawn she finally drifted off. It was almost noon when she woke up.

Maggie was visiting with Judy Hart in the kitchen when Jana found them. In less than five minutes, Jana was sitting at the table, and Maggie was setting eggs topped with cheese, bacon and an English muffin in front of her.

"Eat," the older woman directed, pouring her a glass of milk.

"Where's JT?" Jana found herself blushing as she asked.

"In town," Maggie answered.

"They're tying up everything," Judy added.

"You're staying here on guard?" Jana felt a shudder go through her.

"Just staying here with you. There's no more danger with Kellerman dead, but just until the file is closed, I'm here," Judy assured her.

"When will that be?" Jana asked, wanting it all over.

"Probably sometime tonight or maybe in the morning," Judy went on to explain what was going on. They traced Kellerman's steps. The shooting had been deemed necessary force. Jana was surprised they'd even had to question that it was anything else. She wondered if it was JT's involvement with her that made it questionable.

Judy must have guessed from the look on her face what she was thinking because she assured her. "It's not what you're thinking. It's standard procedure when a gun is discharged by any officer that there's an investigation. This one was very easy because it was so cut and dried. JT has been cleared. Usually it's the police force that does it, but since JT really is the police force here and we're already here it was easy for us to just do it."

Later, Jana helped Tyler with his chores. They were

almost finished when JT showed up. Again, he held himself back from her. By the time Jana headed to bed that night, she couldn't hold in the pain from his withdrawal.

Burying her face in the pillow, she cried, ripped apart by the thought of losing JT and what she thought he felt for her. In her heart, she couldn't blame him for all the trouble she had brought him. She'd endangered his life and his family. She had put him into a position where he was forced to take a man's life.

No, she couldn't blame him for not wanting her around any longer. But it didn't make losing him hurt any less.

The next morning, the Marshals announced they had finished and would be leaving. There were still a few questions of how she was located at the safe house, but they figured that may never be answered, because with Kellerman dead, there was no longer any cause for her to worry.

On the porch, they assured Jana that she could get back to her life. And if there were any further questions, they gave her a number where she could contact them. Jana shook hands with the Marshals as they said good-bye.

Shaking hands with Pete Ferrell, a glimpse of recognition ran through her mind. "Oh, Marshal Ferrell, I remember why I thought I'd met you before. We shared a greeting at Jake's office when I was waiting for Jake and Karen."

"Oh, yes, of course." The man seemed taken back. "I'm sorry, I had forgotten. Good-bye, Miss Hamilton." He turned abruptly, following the others to the car. After they pulled away, Jana turned back to JT, finding him watching her. He turned away and looked out over the pasture.

After they pulled away, Jana turned to JT, finding him watching her. He turned away to look out over the pasture.

When Jana couldn't take it any longer, she spoke. "I guess they're all done."

"Yes," he answered not looking back. "The car you

were driving is the Marshal's so they'll be picking it up at Lou's."

"Yes, I know. Judy told me. I guess I'm stranded."

"You can go with them."

The simple phase burned into her. "You don't need to worry." She came back feeling hurt and anger rise in her. "I'll be moving into town later today, so I won't be in your way. I now have a way to pay for things so you don't need to be concerned. But I think I'll lay down a little while."

Not waiting for him to say anything else, she ran into the house. Instead of heading to the guest room, she headed through the kitchen and out to the barn.

Jana paced up and down in front of the stalls until Daisy nickered for attention. She stopped, running her hand over the horse, easing some of the tension within her, then she moved to visit each of the foals and mares, before making her way to the bale of straw that sheltered the tiny kittens.

The mother cat was with them but showed no sign of concern as she lifted one of the balls of fluff into her lap. On shaky legs, the kitten walked around letting out high pitched meows before cuddling down when she started to stroke it. When she placed the second kitten on her lap, they cuddled together and made a funny little rattle that one day would turn into a purr.

Even though her heart was breaking, Jana managed a smile that dissolved into tears.

"I thought you went in to lie down." The words caught her by surprise. If there would have been a way to disappear, she would have.

Chapter Fifteen

JT had tried to keep his distance from her. When Jana rushed away from him after the marshals left, he figured that was it. Now that she remembered everything, she no longer needed him. He ached inside like he never had before. He tried to convince himself it was for the best, but it did no good. He wanted her in his life.

JT hoped a couple hours of hard labor would ease his soul. He hadn't even made it to the barn when he knew it would be hopeless. Still, he continued on, the chores needed to be done. He picked up the pitch fork just inside the door and went to work.

The first stall was not even finished before he made up his mind he wasn't going to let Jana go without a fight to win her. He would give her time. He wasn't sure how he would manage it, especially with her in Denver, but he would figure out some way to take the time off.

The feeling of peace that came over him took his breath away. Leaning forward, he rested on the pitchfork. The decision was right. Now he just had to figure out how to convince Jana. Taking a deep breath to calm his racing heart, he sensed rather then heard her in the barn.

Following his instincts, he made his way to the back. He saw her almost hidden in the shadows. Her head hung down over her lap and the little balls of fur that she cuddled to her.

"I thought you went in to lie down."

She jerked when he spoke but didn't look up. As he

moved closer, she shifted ever so slightly, putting her back to him. Immediately, he felt a sense of wrongness.

"Jana?" He didn't like the way she moved, cutting him out. Three quick strides brought him to her. He caught her chin, and though she resisted, he forced it up.

The tears on her cheeks dissipated any resolve he might have had left of giving her space. "Jana." He dropped to his knees. "Oh, baby, what's wrong?" He slid his arms around her.

The sob that escaped her made it difficult to understand the, "I'm sorry."

JT felt his heart drop. She was going to leave him. Pain hit so hard he almost didn't catch the next words that tumbled out amidst the tears.

"I understand why you don't want me. I could've gotten Ty killed. I brought you so much trouble ...." She kept going on about the trouble she caused, but his mind had focused on three words, "don't want me".

"Don't want you?" he cut her off, tilting her face up, forcing her to look at him. "Don't want you?" he repeated louder now that he had her attention. "You thought that? Oh baby, you got it all wrong. I want you so much it's killing me just thinking of you leaving."

"You don't want me to go?" Her eyes were wide and he could see her lips trembling. "After all the trouble I caused −"

He cut her off again, this time with his lips. She surrendered to him with a hunger that was explosive. He was about to come totally apart when his mind got in the way, telling him they needed to settle a few things first.

"Oh, sweetheart." He broke the kiss, resting his forehead against her. "I don't think we better do that again just now."

"Why?" Her question was so innocent it almost did him in.

"Trust me." He groaned when the look in her eyes said

just how much she did. Forcing back the urge to kiss her again, he continued. "Because we have something we need to cover." He tried to be logical. "Jana," he paused and took a breath. "I need to know. Do you love me?"

"Yes."

Her answer so simple and so emphatic he let out some of the breath he was holding. "I need you to be sure that it isn't just generated by feelings of fear, loneliness, gratitude or hero worship because of all you've been through. I need to know how you feel about me now that you remember all of your life."

"I love you," she said simply. "It doesn't have anything to do with those things. It has to do with the man you are and how I feel. My past, or any of those things, doesn't affect that. If anything, they probably make it stronger because I know you're the kind of man I always wanted and have been waiting for. I love you."

He wanted to kiss her again. Instead, he reached up and brushed away a tear. "Do you love me enough to give up your life there and move to a small town in Wyoming to be a rancher's and a sheriff's wife?"

"Yes, yes, and yes." This time she kissed him. When she sat back, he felt dazed. "JT, there are things you don't know about me."

"I know what's important. I love you." He recaptured her lips again only to be disturbed by a faint meow. "I think we better put these guys down before we drop them."

Jana laughed, picking one up and brushing her cheek against it, while JT reached for the other, returning it to its mother. He then smiled at her and brushed back her hair. "Well, I did it partly right. I'm at least on my knees when I proposed. Though, I don't have a ring here to give you."

She wrapped her arms around his neck, joining him on the ground instead of him making it off his knees. "You did it perfectly. I'm not worried about the ring."

"Umm, sweetheart," he said between nibbling kisses

on her lips, along her chin, under her ear, and back. He forced himself to stop, pushing her away. "I have to ask you one important thing about your past and I need to know the answer."

"Yes," she sighed bringing another groan from deep in his throat.

"Before you said you didn't think you had ever made love before. I need to know."

She bit the edge of the bottom of her lip, swollen from his kisses, and if she wasn't already flushed, he would have bet she was blushing.

Her head shook slowly. "I ... I haven't ever." Then, as if needing to explain, she continued. "I was the ultimate good girl during the time I passed the mad, teenage, everyone-does-it phase. Then, I realized it was important to me to wait for the right man, and he didn't come along until now. I know the man I've been waiting for is you. I love you. No fear or hero worship, just plain what I feel inside about you."

"Thank you. I love you, too." He kissed her nose and stood, reaching for her hand.

"JT?"

"We're waiting."

"But –"

He cut her off with a shake of his head and a quick kiss. "This is important. We wait until we're married."

"When?"

He grinned. "Well, how about right now? If we hurry, we could get a license before they close tonight. Then we can call over to the church. I know I'm hurrying you, but I still want it nice. In fact, I'm changing it to tomorrow morning, ten o'clock. That will give us some more time." The appeal in his face must have been enough to sway her because she just laughed.

"Yes." There was no doubt in her answer.

They sealed it with a kiss that again almost got out of

hand.

"I think we'd better get out of the barn and go see what my son and aunt think."

"How do you think Tyler will take this?"

"Ty will think it's great. He loves you, maybe as much as I do, but you're mine. I'm the one that found you first." He slid his arm around her, tucking her to his body. "We've got a lot of planning to do."

JT's arm was still around Jana as they walked into the house a few minutes later. Maggie took one look at them and declared. "It's about time."

Tyler shot up from the couch in the family room studying them a second before pumping his arm in the air in a victory motion. "Yes."

JT raised an eyebrow at his son's reaction. "What has you so happy?"

"You're going to marry Jana," Ty answered back without any hesitation.

"Really and how do you know that?"

"Dad," the boy drew out in exasperation, making it clear that it was only obvious, then again maybe it was.

"I take it, it's okay with you?" Jana asked.

"Yeah, I think you'll make a great mom."

With that tears blossomed in Jana's eyes, she left JT's side to go hug his son. "I love you," she whispered into Ty's hair, pressing a kiss to his head.

JT met Maggie's eyes.

"This one is right." His aunt's voice was hushed as she wiped away a tear.

JT felt his own emotions rise watching the two people he loved most in the world. "Hey, how do I get on this?" He crossed the room, wrapping his arms around them both.

They stood like that for several minutes forming a family unit.

"Well," the older woman snuffled. "When are we planning this for? Or have you decided yet?"

"Ten o'clock tomorrow morning," JT answered.

"Ten, tomorrow." The woman repeated stunned.

"When it's right." He shrugged and Jana blushed in his arms.

"Wow," Tyler exclaimed.

"We're going to go see about the license now. Then we'll call and arrange the church," JT said.

"I'll tell you what." Maggie held up a hand to stop him. "I'll make the call, but how about we change the time to noon, and that will give us more time to set things up for the morning.

JT looked at Jana, and when she nodded, he agreed. "Okay, ready to go?" As they walked out of the door, he caught sight of Maggie reaching for the phone. "Something tells me this wedding might not be as small and plain as we thought."

"What? How so?"

"Let's just say; I know my aunt. In fact, if you have a preference of flowers, you might want to go back and tell her now."

Jana shook her head and laughed.

JT figured she didn't realize how serious he was.

Jana still couldn't believe they were able to get a marriage license, because she didn't have any identification, though she now remembered her social security number. It ended up there were some advantages, when you were marrying the sheriff, and had a call from an FBI agent to confirm your identity and fax a copy of your driver's license.

They were driving back through town when Jana saw the sign of Ruth's boutique and laid her hand on JT's arm. "I'd like to get a nice dress to wear."

"No problem. I should have thought of it." He turned at the corner to go around back. "You'll need some money." He reached for his wallet.

"I have some in my bank account, but it may be a

while until I can get to it."

"It doesn't matter. What's mine is yours."

Jana was already riding the warmth of love, but his words fired a whole new spark. There was no stopping the need to lean over and kiss him. "I'm a very lucky lady."

His arms wrapped around her to keep her tight against him. "I'm feeling kind of lucky myself." He nuzzled her neck. A horn blasted behind them. JT sat back smiling. "Trying to neck in town when you're the sheriff is not easy."

Jana was still laughing when he came around to open the door for her.

"While you shop, I have a few errands to run. So take your time, and I'll meet you there." He walked her to the door of the boutique.

"Hi," Jana greeted Ruth as she stepped in.

"Congratulations," Ruth answered back to her surprise.

"What?"

"That you and JT were just over at the county getting a marriage license? Please, I have my sources. I don't have any wedding dresses, but I do have a couple of very nice dresses." She led her through the store. "I have one I think you'll like. I already put it in a dressing room, with a couple others."

Jana was in shock at how fast word had gotten out as she walked to the dressing room. The woman was right when she showed her the calf length, white dress, the choice was easy. She fell in love with it as soon as she slid it on.

·"I'd say JT will like that," Ruth said in approval when Jana stepped out to show her. "What do you think?"

"Perfect. Now for some shoes."

"Not going to wear your tennis shoes?"

"Not this time. I want JT to see me at my best."

"The way that man looked at you the other day, I think he already likes what he sees. Still, a little high-heeled sandal will show your legs off great."

Jana almost laughed when the dress and shoes cost more than what she had spent on all she bought a couple days earlier, but she shrugged. This was special. There was only one thing she was sad about. The nightgown that caught her eye the other day was no longer there.

⋘⋙

JT went to the jewelry store. Once he had the size from the ring that was in Jana's jewelry bag, it didn't take him long to choose a ring set. The round, three-quarter diamond, mounted in a combination white and yellow gold setting had two small chips on either side. It was classic, but different. Enough to get an awe but not ostentatious, which was Jana, beautiful, but not in a showy way, like her true beauty, which came from her inner core. He knew a lot of people would crow if they heard him say something poetic like that.

JT entered Ruth's just as the woman was handing Jana a garment bag. "Ready."

"Actually, I have one more stop I'd like to make if that's all right."

"Sure, in fact, I thought of something else I need to get."

"All right, meet you at the truck in half an hour."

"Fine by me. Why don't I take this," he took the bags from her, "to the truck for you?"

"No peeking."

"Scouts honor." He raised his hand in a pledge.

Jana stretched up to kiss his cheek before hurrying out the door.

"She's good for you," Ruth said from behind the counter.

"I think so." JT watched Jana disappear from in front of the window before turning back to Ruth. "What I'm wondering, do you still happen to have that nightgown Jana was looking at the other day?"

196

"As a matter fact, I do." She reached under the counter and drew out a silver wrapped package with glittering ribbons. "I knew you'd be back for it." She laid it in front of him.

JT laughed, pulling out his wallet. "How much do I owe you?" He laid the money on the counter. "Thanks, Ruth. Keep the change."

After putting the packages in the truck, he still had twenty minutes before meeting Jana, but the pharmacy caught his eye. It had been a long time since he had bought condoms, and he felt slightly embarrassed as he walked in the store, but he figured everyone in town would know what he'd be doing tomorrow night.

The thought of Jana getting pregnant made him pause. They hadn't talked about it. He liked the thought, but after his first wife, he wasn't going to assume.

Jana liked Tyler. There was no doubt about that, and though he would like to have more children, Tyler would be enough if Jana didn't want them. So he endured the small talk and knowing smiles as he paid for an economy package of condoms.

Cಚಿೋಲ

Jana hadn't visited the jewelry store on her first shopping trip to town, but she remembered walking by it. Mr. Grover was a slightly built man with wire spectacles. He greeted her the minute she walked into the door. He didn't even wait before he directed her to the wedding bands for men.

"JT was just in here a minute ago. Don't ask me what he got because I'm not telling, but it was one of my personal favorites."

She gave a little laugh then shifted, feeling a little awkward. "Before I look at them, I should tell you, I only have thirty dollars to put down on a ring, and it will probably be at least a week before I can get to my bank account."

197

The man waved her comment away. "I'm not worried about that. Everyone in town has heard about the murderer after you. Who knows, maybe I'll have you do my taxes to work it off. Anybody that can make sense of Lou's has to be good."

"If you'd like, I'd love to."

"Then let's get down to looking at rings."

The ring she chose had a small diamond chip in the center of a star that reminded her of a sheriff's badge so much she knew it was for him.

JT was just crossing the street when she reached the truck.

"All ready?" she greeted him.

"Oh yeah," he said, opening the door for her. When she went to get in, he pinned her between the metal and his body, taking her mouth by storm. For almost a minute she returned the kiss with eagerness then pushed back.

"Oh, my," her heart was racing. She put her hands to her heated cheeks. "JT, we're on the street." She glanced up and down the block so guiltily that JT started to laugh.

"Then let's get you off the street." If possible, her blush grew brighter. She hurriedly climbed into the truck.

ᚢᛉᛊᚢ

JT headed for the barn while Jana took her dress in the house and hung it in her closet before going to find Maggie in the kitchen. "Need any help?"

"Nope. Dinner's just some things from the freezer. How'd everything go?"

"We're all set. We have the license, and I found a dress and a ring for JT. I just can't believe it. I've waited and looked all over for a man to love and then, with all that's been happening, I can hardly believe it's real. Maggie, I really do love him." She looked out the window at the man who had her heart.

"I know you do, and he loves you. It was easy to see it before either of you even recognized it."

Jana smiled at Maggie's words, watching father and son working together. She had come to love them both in such a short time. She hoped her and Tyler could continue their relationship like it was, that he could accept her as a friend, and maybe a mother. Ty said he thought she'd make a great mother. She wanted it to be true.

Unconsciously, her hand went to her stomach, and she wondered if she'd ever carry JT's child there. They hadn't talked about children. He was such a terrific father, but he already had Tyler, and his experience with Tyler's mother wasn't the best, but he was taking a chance again on love and marriage, maybe he'd take a chance again on children. She was definitely not like his ex-wife. Jana would love to carry his child.

"I'm going to help the guys with chores," she called over her shoulder, heading for the door.

Tyler was the first to see her, but when Jana held up a finger to her lips, he kept quiet as she snuck up behind JT. Just as she was about to get him, he spun around and grabbed her. Jana jumped and squealed.

Tyler doubled over with laughter.

JT puller her close and whispered in her ear. "You can't sneak up on me, darling. My body goes on overload every time you're near. I want you."

"Oh," was all Jana could get out, looking into his eyes steamy with desire. She knew what he meant. She felt the same way, like the air was electrified. Still, she gathered all her sassiness and pushed back. "I came to help."

"You did," he grinned.

Jana figured it was a statement and not a question and turned in a quick action that flipped her hair out behind her. JT roared in laughter, but she ignored him, sauntering over to Ty.

"Let's put her to work Ty," JT said behind her. "What do you think, mucking out the stalls?"

She glanced back over her shoulder, "Ha, ha." But she

picked up a pair of gloves and the pitchfork. The light mood continued for the next twenty-five minutes while they worked together.

"All done, dad," Ty called out, closing Daisy's stall.

"All right, why don't you head in and wash up."

"I'm done, too," Jana said as Tyler left.

"You come here a minute." JT's order had a huskiness about it that had Jana eager to follow as he led her to the back of the barn. "Sit."

She settled on what was becoming her favorite bale of straw. She was surprised when he dropped down to his knee.

"I didn't have this to give to you before, but I think it's fitting if I still give it to you here. In fact, if I didn't want you in my bed so bad tomorrow, I'd be tempted to make love to you for the first time out here."

Jana knew he was teasing, but there was also a little truth in the words. For some unknown reason, this had become their spot. Still, her heart jumped when he reached into his pocket and pulled out a small ring box.

"You've had a while to think about it now, so I'm asking you again. Jana, will you marry me?"

Tears once more misted her eyes, but they didn't dim her smile. "Yes, oh, yes," she said, as he slid the ring on her finger. "Oh my, it's beautiful." She gasped. Staring at it a second before she threw her arms around his neck to let her kisses express her feelings.

The rest of the evening they were well chaperoned by Tyler, Maggie and Doc, who had joined them. Jana asked Doc if he would give her away. Tyler was going to be the best man, since Malcolm couldn't make it back into town. Maggie, of course, would be matron.

Chapter Sixteen

Pulling in front of the church just before noon, JT knew he had been right. Though it had been planned fast, and they were keeping it simple, it was far from plain.

It looked like the whole town was there, and he guessed they cleaned out the entire flower shop. The ladies in town had obviously been busy since sunrise. The way into the church was lined with white hooks that looked like shepherd's staffs with bouquets and ribbons tied on them.

"Wow," Tyler commented beside him.

"My thoughts exactly," JT agreed.

"Aunt Maggie was on the phone most of yesterday while you were gone."

"I can tell."

"You upset?" Tyler turned to his father.

"No, I'm flattered that everyone would think enough to go to all this trouble. I just hope Jana isn't overwhelmed. Everyone is still a stranger to her."

"Jana loves us, and she loves the town. She told that the day at the park." There was certainty in his voice, but it was gone on the next sentence. "Dad, do you think Jana would let me call her mom?"

JT's throat thickened with emotion, and he had trouble getting the words out. "If you'd like to, why don't you ask her?" He placed his hand on his son's shoulder as they made their way into the church, accepting well wishes on the way from everyone close enough to the aisle to greet him.

He took his position at the front and was relieved when he looked back and saw Maggie was smiling at the back of the chapel. That meant Jana was here and all was well. They had kept him from seeing her all morning, and he had longed to see her.

When the prelude music started to play, he turned with Tyler to watch expectantly at the back doors. The music changed and another wave of anticipation hit. He was like a man dying of thirst to see her, but he wasn't prepared for the sight.

He thought she looked good in anything, but could hardly believe he was marrying the woman on Doc's arm. The simple flowing dress whispered of every curve. The pure white color screamed of the gift of innocence she was giving to him. But it was the love that sparkled in her eyes that took his breath. It was there, open, for all to see, and testified of the years of happiness to come.

The only time her eyes left his, was to look to his son. For a second, her face gentled, the smile remained, but JT recognized it as a loving acceptance that said to her, he was her son now.

CB&O

Jana clutched the bouquet of white calla lilies, yellow tulips and blue hyacinths that Maggie had handed her. She was unbelievably nervous when she saw all the people. Then her eyes found JT and that was all she saw, except for a brief look to Tyler, who, like his father was dressed in a suit. Her heart filled with joy. Whether Tyler felt like it yet or not, in her heart, he was her son as much as if he had come from her body.

Her eyes went back to JT's. He was waiting. He was her future. Everything passed pretty much in a blur, then he was sliding his ring on her finger and she slid hers on his. He looked pleased when he saw it, and then he took her mouth in the sealing kiss.

Outside on the back lawn, a reception had been set up.

People mingled, congratulated, and ate the potluck the town's people put together. Several times Jana turned to him with tears of pleasure in her eyes from the love the town showed for him and feeling lucky to be part of it.

JT made it through an hour and a half before he decided he was ready to kidnap his wife for some private time. Jana was talking to Ruth and a couple other ladies so he excused himself to find Maggie.

Maggie met him crossing the lawn. "You ready to go?" she asked him first.

"Yeah, I know we didn't talk about this but could you give us a couple hours alone?"

"Actually, Tyler and I are spending the night at Doc's. That will give you a little time for a honeymoon, until you can get away for a real one. We can take care of the chores if you want to go to Denver and pick up Jana's things. I know your deputies have worked up a schedule to cover you for the next few days."

"You think of everything. Thanks." He gave his aunt a hug.

"You're welcome. I guess I ought to tell you now that I'm going to be moving out in a couple weeks."

"Moving out?"

Maggie held up her hand to cut him off. "Now, don't start. You two need time to start your new life together, and besides the way you look at her, it won't be long before you start filling up all the rooms of that big house with babies."

JT shifted uncomfortably. "I don't know if Jana wants children. She loves Tyler and that's enough for me."

Maggie laughed. "That little lady wants to carry your baby so much, that if it happens tonight, correction this afternoon on her first time," she smiled wickedly, "she wouldn't be happier."

JT smiled a little at the thought but was still uncertain. "You still don't have to go. Jana wouldn't want you to."

"Oh, I'm not going far. I thought I'd have a wedding of my own."

"Doc."

"He's been after me for a couple years, and I thought now was about time I said yes. I was going to this summer anyway. I figured you two could take care of yourselves. Now, I don't have to worry."

"You should have said something."

"I wasn't ready yet. Besides, I wouldn't have missed a day helping you raise Tyler."

"I love you." He gave the woman who had given up so much of her life for him and his son another hug.

"And I you, my boy." She smiled, raising her hand to touch his cheek. "Now go get your bride."

JT didn't need any more encouragement. By the time he and Jana found Ty and said their good-byes, people lined the path to the car. At the car, they paused long enough for Jana to throw her bouquet and JT to give her one last kiss for the cheering crowd.

"That was the most wonderful wedding." Jana beamed as they drove away.

"I'm sorry your brother couldn't be there or any of your friends."

"That's okay, and he'll understand and come visit when he gets back in the states."

"Not feeling overwhelmed?" JT couldn't stop from asking what had concerned him, though she seemed to have been having a good time.

"I loved it. Everyone cares for you so much."

"Are you going to start crying on me?"

"Possibly. Every woman is allowed to cry on her wedding day."

JT wondered if she was as nervous as he was. He wanted her so badly, the thought of the ten minute drive home was agony. What was worse was he had been celibate a long time, and he wanted to make the first time for her special, but he felt like a randy, hormone-driven teenager.

Jana shifted in the seat. She'd been nervous and excited all day. They were on their way home. The idea felt great and funny. Her home with JT, and they were going to make love. She hoped he wouldn't be disappointed. As if he sensed her unease, he reached over, caught her fingers and brought them to his lips.

She squeezed his hand, looking over. "Would you think that I'm silly if I said that I was nervous?"

"Not in the least."

"I want to make love with you." Her honest statement jolted through him.

"Sweetheart, you should not say things like that when I still have two miles of road to concentrate on."

Jana's little laugh told him she didn't know how serious he was. He fought to keep his focus on the road though every cell of his body was aware of her next to him. He pulled up to the front of the house not bothering with the garage.

JT took a deep steadying breath on his way around the car in an effort to slow down his raging desire, but the moment her feet hit the ground, his control failed. He swung her up into his arms. Her outcry was stifled by his mouth in a kiss that didn't break as he carried her up the steps.

"JT." She managed to get out, but it wasn't a protest as her arms locked around his neck.

"Every bride deserves to be carried over the threshold," he managed to get out against her lips, as he fumbled for the key, while wondering why he had to be so responsible and lock the thing.

Jana finally took the key and helped him with the lock, then once inside, reached back to catch the frame so she could turn the deadbolt.

It was JT's turn to break the kiss. "Believe me,

sweetheart, if that's for me, you don't have to worry about locking me in. I have no desire to leave you."

"We don't have a 'do not disturb sign'."

"Only a fool with a death wish would disturb me now." He gave her another firm kiss. "I promised myself to be patient, but I want to make love to you."

"Yes." Was Jana's answer, pulling his mouth back down to hers.

JT wasn't sure how he made it to his room. He lowered her down on the bed, knocking the wrapped package off the bed. "That was a present for you, one I dreamed of taking off you, but I'm going to fantasize of this dress forever."

"I dreamed of you, too." Her words were breathless, but there was a wobble in her voice that he guessed was nervousness.

Reigning in his desire, he pulled back trying to give her time to adjust. "Jana, I want you to promise to tell me if I do anything that makes you uncomfortable. You have to promise it. I want this to be beautiful for you."

"I love you."

"Promise."

"I promise, but I don't feel uncomfortable. I feel … incredible."

"You haven't seen anything yet." He proceeded to show her all the things she had been waiting for, and proving, it was worth the wait.

03&0

Jana came out of sleep with the feel of JT's hand stroking up and down her back. She stretched enjoying the feel of his body alongside of hers. Her cheek rested on his chest. She turned her head slightly to press her lips over his heart. She felt him kiss the top of her head.

"You make me forget my age." His voice was low and husky.

Jana couldn't hold back the laughter that bubbled up inside her. "Is it always going to be this way between us?"

"If it is, it's going to kill me, but what a way to go."

Laughter rolled out again, and she swatted his chest.

"You think we should finally get up?" he asked, catching her hand, laying it back on his chest under his own.

"I'm starving." She pressed up to meet his eyes.

"I was hoping you would say that."

It was almost three-quarters of an hour before they made it into the kitchen. With JT's help, Jana found it took twice as long to make a sandwich, but it was a whole lot more fun. Even pouring a glass of milk was a challenge when he came up behind her, slid his arms around her, and nuzzled her neck.

"What would you like to do now?" JT asked and took the last bite of his sandwich.

Jana thought for a moment. "Go horseback riding."

"Are you sure you're up for it?"

Jana felt the blush warm her cheeks. "Yes."

He stood and held out his hand. "As you wish."

Jana let him pull her up in his arms. "Have I told you lately that I love you?"

"Not for the past twenty minutes."

"Then it's about time I did again. I love you." She stretched up to kiss him.

He slid his fingers into her hair, holding her head while he feasted on her mouth.

He broke off abruptly. "No more or you won't get your ride."

Smiling, Jana hooked her arm around his waist, dragging him to the door. "I didn't think I could ever be this happy," she said a few minutes later when they were headed across the field on horseback. "Two weeks ago, I thought I was going to die, and now, all my dreams are coming true."

"What other dreams do you have?" He reached over and caught her hand from off the saddle-horn to rub his thumb over her knuckles. When she hesitated, he maneuvered his horse so their legs brushed, and he brought her hands to his lips. "Tell me, my love, so I can make them come true."

When she lifted her eyes, they were filled with emotion and when she started to talk, the words flowed from her. "We haven't talked about this, and I know you have Tyler. You raised him yourself, and it would be like starting over for you." She stopped.

His lips twitched slightly. "Are you trying to tell me you'd like to have a baby?" He could hardly believe it. Maggie had been right. He should have known. Jana was nothing like his first wife who he'd married thinking of having a family, which wasn't to be, and now all he wanted from Jana was her, and she was giving him one of his heart's desires.

"It doesn't have to be now, if you'd just think about it. I hadn't been really feeling like my maternal clock was ticking, and I still don't. It's just, I guess with the things that have happened to me lately, they kind of stressed what was important in life. And …"

She seemed to run out of steam, but JT didn't care. He got everything he needed to know for now. "Jana," he again brought her hand to his lips. "I'd love to give you a baby. Growing up as an only child, I always wanted a big family. It was just, after Tyler's mother, I learned all women didn't want that, but believe me, I'd love to see you with my child."

Luckily, the horses had stopped because Jana launched herself from her saddle, throwing her arms around his neck. JT caught her and pulled her over his lap to receive her response. When their lips parted, he leaned his forehead against hers.

"You know, unless you got something from Doc, you could already be pregnant. I planned to protect you, but I kind of got caught up in you and forgot." He kissed her nose and then her lips when they made a perfect little O. He smiled. "Believe me, I'll do all I can to see your dreams come true."

०३४०

The barnyard was quiet when they guided the horses back in. It was to be expected but an uneasy feeling settled on JT. His glanced around, not seeing anything out of the ordinary, but his gut tightened. His instincts shifted to full alert, and he knew danger.

"Why don't you go in and fix a snack while I take care of the horses," he suggested as he dismounted, looking around for trouble.

"I can help." She joined him on the ground.

"No, in fact, let me walk you to the house." He took her elbow, curving his body around hers.

The tension in his body was unmistakable, but what bothered Jana the most was the feeling of déjà vu. "What's wrong?"

"What makes you think −" he stopped, knowing he wasn't fooling her and was not going to lie. "Something's not right," he whispered.

"It feels like it did when Jake was walking me to the safe house."

"Come on." He changed direction, pulling her around the side of the house.

"JT, you don't think? Kellerman's dead." She followed his motions, crouching low and keeping close to the wall.

"Yeah, but the question nobody seemed to answer was, how Kellerman knew where the safe house was? The bomb had to be set ahead of time. No way did he follow you there, get in the house, and set it."

"And then get up to the hillside to shoot at us." She continued on with his thoughts.

"Exactly."

A shiver went through her.

JT stopped peering around the corner then motioned to

her to sprint with him to one of the sheds. Reaching it, they pressed against the wall while JT tried to scan the area.

"But why would they come after me now that Kellerman's gone?" she asked.

"Maybe honoring the hit," he paused. "Or maybe you saw who it was," he hypothesized, checking around the corner.

"I didn't see anyone."

"Maybe they don't know that." Reaching for her hand, he drew her with him behind the next shed and hunkered down behind it. "Who were all the people you had contact with during your time in custody?"

"No one. I only was allowed to make a few calls. Mostly, I did emails, and I was always very cautious not to say anything about where I was."

"But someone knew."

"Jake said there were only four people who knew where we were going. Jake and Karen made the arrangements personally and cleared it with the two top guys. I only spoke to a half-dozen marshals. With the first team I had, one went on vacation, and her partner had trouble with an ulcer. Jake and Karen were with me the whole time after that."

"Okay, who else?'

"The head guys are Matthews and Gage and then I saw Pete Ferrell before and that's about all I can put a name to."

"Where'd you meet Ferrell?"

"I saw him in Jake's office. He was looking for some paperwork when I went in there to wait for Jake and Karen."

JT muttered something under his breath that might have been a curse. "I need to get to my gun. I want you to stay down behind the tractor over there." He motioned to about ten feet away.

"You really think someone is here?"

"Yeah, I do."

"I want to stay with you."

He ran his hand over her cheek in a quick caress. "Look, it might be nothing, but, I need to know you're out of the way and safe while I check it out." He could see the worry written over her face. "Trust me."

The two simple words were all it took. With a nod, she pressed her lips firmly against his. "Be careful," she choked out. Crouching low, she scurried to the tractor.

JT watched her get settled. A touch of pride filled him at her unquestioning faith in him and his instincts.

When she was well under, JT peered around the corner again. Coast clear, he crouched and ran for the house. The shot rang out from the barn loft when he was halfway across the yard. Dust kicked up inches from his feet. JT ducked and dodged.

The next shot whizzed past his head, another followed him as he dove behind the huge cottonwood that sat on the corner of the lawn. JT pressed his back against the bark as he drew in a deep breath.

He was in trouble, pinned down, no weapon and fifty feet to the house. The distance never seemed greater. Even if he made it to the house, he wasn't sure if he dared opened the door. They had been gone long enough that, if he didn't miss his guess, Ferrell had plenty of time to rig an explosive like the one that destroyed the safe house. His best bet would be the garage and his spare gun in the lock box in his patrol vehicle.

Stretching his head out one side, he pulled back an instant before the bullet burrowed into the tree. It was like the starting gun at a track meet. JT was off, zigzagging his way toward the garage. A bullet slammed into the side of the garage.

He made it to the door just as another shot sounded. JT jerked and stumbled at the burning sensation on his thigh. He didn't stop to look down to see where he was hit. The pain and stickiness told him that. Instinct or wishful thinking told him it was just a graze.

His hand was on the doorknob when the next shot hit his shoulder, knocking him into the door. It flew open. JT fell, hitting the cement floor with bone jarring force. Pain ricocheted through his body until his head impacted with the floor, and everything fell away into darkness.

⋘⋙

JT had just disappeared when the first shot rang out. His name broke from her lips in an agonizing gasp. Her instinct was to run after him. Only knowing he would want her to stay put kept her in place. She flinched at the second shot.

"No, please." It seemed like she was pleading for protection a lot lately, but this time, it was for JT. Her heart felt like it was going to stop when she heard the next shot followed almost immediately by another.

Jana held her breath, waiting for the next. She almost thought there weren't going to be any more when the next three shots came in rapid succession. Locking her jaw to keep herself from screaming, Jana was unable to stay put any longer. She crawled from under the tractor, making it to the corner where JT had disappeared.

She peeked around the side of the building, but there was no sign of JT or the shooter. Panic threatened to send her racing after him. With a great amount of effort, logic won out.

Jana crept to the other corner and peered around. She pulled back quickly, the open pasture offered no hiding places. Think, she told herself then noticed the propped open window that gave her a chance of getting into the shed.

Making her way to the window, her heart about sank when she tried to shove it up further, and it wouldn't budge. Desperately, she worked her head and shoulders inside until she managed to grab a hook and pull herself up. It was a tight fit and her body threatened to get stuck. But, after a lot of wiggling, she dropped, panting, amidst the tools on the work bench.

Fear ran through her body, but she didn't let it slow her. Sliding cautiously to the floor, she crossed to the door. The window was covered by a thick film of dirt that gave everything a cloudy, unreal appearance. Still, she could see most of the yard from the barn to the house.

There was no sign of JT. Concern for him warred against logic of staying put. Logic was starting to lose out when Jana caught a movement out of the corner of her eye. She shifted to get a better look. She couldn't make out the man's features under the baseball cap, but knew it wasn't JT. Jana dodged back closer to the frame as the man moved into the open.

He stopped in the middle of the yard and looked her direction then toward the house a second before turning to the shed. Jana pressed against the wall. Her eyes darted around the murky interior. Jana grabbed a branding iron hanging to the right of her head. Gripping it in both hands, she held it high like a bat.

Her heart pounded in her chest. She was afraid any moment the door would swing open, but she was even more afraid of what had happened to JT. There was no way he would have let the man walk free out into the yard if he had been able to stop him. Tears filled Jana's eyes. She tried to blink them back, willing herself to remain calm, to concentrate, to listen. Telling herself she had to focus, that would be the only way she could help JT.

Jana flinched back as a shadowed form crossed in front of the window. Her breath caught as she waited for the door to open. Instead, a second later, the shape passed the other window, moving around the corner where the tractor stood.

The next two minutes passed like hours. It was the crackling of dried weeds left from fall that alerted her to the gunman just outside the window she'd climbed through. Jana ducked down behind the work bench, pressed herself into the small space and listened.

More weeds crackled, grass swished, and he was gone. Uncertain whether to stay or move, the decision was taken from her a moment later when a shadow flickered across the floor. The man passed the window she had been staring out.

Adrenaline was pumping heavy in her veins as she eyed the door. Jana watched as the knob turned and chided herself for not trying to lock it. Sliding silently across the floor, she came up next to the framing, the branding iron positioned high over her head.

Fear and anger speared through her body as the door creaked open. Her heart raced. She stood ready, knowing she would have to strike. She had to get the man. She had to find JT.

Thoughts of her love brought tears back to her eyes, making objects swim. Jana blinked rapidly to bring things into focus as his head cleared the door. Instinct took over. She swung out with all her might.

The strike was low, missing his head. It impacted solidly on his arm and chest. The man let out an agonizing cry. A shot burst from the gun, threatening to deafen her before it dropped to the floor. The man's arm hung limp at his side. Jana was raising the iron for another swing when the door hit her, slamming her into the bench.

A cry escaped her, but she didn't let the jolt slow her. She came up swinging. This time, the man was ready. Grabbing her wrist in a bruising hold, he brought her hand down against the corner of the workbench with three sharp blows. Jana let out a cry of pain as the branding iron fell from her fingers.

In a blink of an eye, the hand released her wrist and locked around her throat, squeezing down, cutting off her air. The hard body pressed her back over the workbench. All her struggles yielded nothing.

The pressure tightened. Her ears began to ring and her

mind went fuzzy, but she still recognized the U.S. Marshal. She clawed at Ferrell's hand, but her movements lost their strength. Her arms became heavy and sluggish.

"I was trying to make this quick … and painless." The voice was raspy in her ear. "I didn't want to have to kill Termaine. You just had to stay together."

Jana tried to scream out, but no air would pass his fingers. JT couldn't be dead.

"Like Kellerman, I couldn't let you live. You saw me that day in Jake's office. If you mentioned it again to someone, they might have put it together."

Darkness spread over her. One last time, her heart cried out for JT, knowing her loving him brought his death. She hated letting Ferrell win, but without JT, it didn't matter.

The roar that burst in her ears shook her whole world. She felt herself fall. Rough wood scraped against her body. Air rushed back into her lungs, but it was too late to care.

ೞ

From the doorway, JT watched Jana follow the hired killer to the ground. With the gun still in his hand, he stumbled across the room. He fell, as much as knelt, beside the pair. He wasn't surprised to see Ferrell or that he couldn't find a pulse. His shot had been close range, and even though his body shook from shock and loss of blood, the shot had been true. Instantly, he forgot the man, turning his attention to Jana.

She lay as still as the dead man. Pain ripped through his heart. Tears of gratitude broke free when his fingers found flutters of life.

"Jana," he choked out, letting her know he was there. In the distance, he heard the sirens of his deputies approaching. With his uninjured arm, he took her hand, interlocking their fingers as he waited.

Epilogue

The antiseptic smell hung in the air as Jana walked down the hospital hallway. Her fingers were interlocked in JT's. His limp had disappeared along with the sling on his arm. For the first couple weeks of marriage, they were a sad looking pair, he with a crutch and a sling, she with one arm in a cast from Ferrell breaking it against the workbench. Still, life couldn't be any better as far as Jana was concerned.

Sneaking a sideways glance at her husband, she found him watching her and returned his smile. His fingers gave hers a little squeeze. Stopping outside the closed door, JT knocked then opened it as bid.

"Hi," Jana greeted the man sitting up in the chair. He still looked pale, but considering Jake had almost died, had spent over three weeks in a coma, and another three here in the hospital, he looked pretty good.

"Howdy," Jake's voice rang with his ever present drawl. He held out his hand to JT.

"We're heading out and wanted to say good-bye."

"So you got the last of your stuff all loaded and ready to settle in the wilds of Wyoming with your lawman." There was approval in his words.

"Yep," Jana tried to add a little accent of her own for the Texan. "We have to get back for Maggie's wedding, and my brother's going to be flying in to meet everyone. We heard they're going to spring you."

"Finally and there's a pretty little nurse here that's

agreed to come by and keep an eye on me. Not too bad for an old banged-up cowboy. I might even see if I can talk her into comin' up to visit. That is, if you promise us a horseback ride."

"I think we can arrange that and a Dutch oven dinner to go with it," JT answered.

"That sounds pretty promisin'."

"Take care, Jake." Jana leaned over to kiss his cheek. "Thank you for saving my life."

"Augh, I only helped a little." The man actually blushed. "You saved yourself again, darlin', and came out right good for it."

Jana's eyes followed his look to JT and glowed with pleasure. "I sure did. And believe me. I plan to enjoy the future I have."

"Sound like a good idea." Jake nodded.

"I agree with that." JT brought her hand up behind her back to bring her to him so he could seal the statement with a kiss.

"Be seeing you, Jake." JT drew her out.

"Thanks again," Jana said one last time before heading for the door.

"Newlyweds."

They heard his laughter follow them from the room, but it wasn't what stopped them. In unison, they turned to each other. "To the future," JT growled out the words in promise.

"Yes," Jana said, as she sealed it with a kiss.

About the Author

I grew up in a small town in Wyoming loving the outdoors, sports, art, and reading Hardy Boys books. After reading them all at least a half dozen times, I started writing my own stories.

Thirty years ago I married a wonderful, honorable man. I have five children and eleven grandchildren. I love traveling. Through my husband's work and vacations, I have visited much of the United States, all over Western Europe, Canada, Mexico, China, Thailand, Cambodia and Australia, giving me many intriguing locations and experiences for my stories.

I am a storyteller. I write the classic hero story because I think there's a need for more heroes, love, and adventure in our lives. I'm not out to change the world with my writing; I'm just hoping to make your day a little better.

Hope you enjoy.
Alysia S. Knight

Please feel free to visit me through my website:

www.alysiasknight.com

www.ingramcontent.com/pod-product-compliance
Lightning Source LLC
Chambersburg PA
CBHW032119170626
46808CB00006B/2018